Uncertain Outcomes

Uncertain Outcomes

Where international business and government relations collide

Tom Williams

Copyright @ 2015 Tom Williams
All rights reserved.

ISBN: 1505754356
ISBN 13: 9781505754353
Library of Congress Control Number: 2014922918
CreateSpace Independent Pub. Platform
North Charleston, South Carolina

Preface

ALTHOUGH THE CHARACTERS depicted in this novel are fictitious, the story is based on actual facts representative of a trend which led many American companies to relocate overseas during the past thirty years. This movement led to a loss of jobs in the United States, an escape from restrictive environmental regulations, which had become increasingly onerous, and a loss of tax revenue to states and the federal government, which is estimated to be in the trillions of US dollars.

Following World War II, the United States was the only large industrial country "still standing," which led to its global dominance in many areas of manufacturing. European and Japanese industries were then just beginning to rebuild their industrial strength. At the same time, the Marshall Plan, sponsored and funded by the US government, was intended primarily to rebuild Western Europe as a bulwark against the communist threat from the east. It pumped billions of US dollars into European economies, which greatly accelerated economic recovery, particularly in Germany.

This led to a growing pool of unregulated "Euro dollars" being available to those who offered reasonable assurance of repayment. That, in turn, led to many commodities, particularly coal, oil, and gas, being priced in US dollars because of the easy availability of these funds across national borders.

As American businesses began to seek overseas markets for further expansion, foreign subsidiaries of those American companies began to spring up in most noncommunist countries. A typical large US multinational company would often have several hundred wholly owned subsidiary corporations primarily to handle marketing and related activities. When local competition slowly began to surface, those companies generally tried to take sales from US-based multinationals using obsolete or copycat products at lower prices.

As US factory wages and benefits continued to climb, companies began to seek overseas production locations where costs could be significantly reduced. This was particularly true for products with high labor content, such as automobiles, as opposed to chemicals and other bulk commodities with relatively low labor costs.

The US government sought to support its companies by providing tax incentives to encourage overseas expansion. President Truman's Point Four Program and tax holidays for drug companies in Puerto Rico are examples of early programs intended to support American companies. However, in the early 1960s, the pendulum began to swing in the opposite direction. Stan Surrey, the new Assistant Secretary for Tax Policy under President Kennedy, believed that US companies were getting unjustified tax breaks and were artificially shifting profits to low-tax countries. Thus began a plethora of tax laws and regulations that were intended to "correct" these "abuses" and encourage companies to avoid tax-haven countries.

Other factors were gradually beginning to have an impact upon these multinational companies. Advances in technology and globalization required nimble approaches to stay ahead of competition. Achieving greater economies of scale to drive down unit costs necessitated looking at factory relocations to less developed countries to drive down labor costs, reduce the costs of environmental compliance and cut tax burdens. Falling trade barriers were opening more and more countries to foreign competition. With the collapse of the Soviet Union many countries began to shed their stodgy state owned businesses in favor of privatization which was now recognized as a more efficient approach. The formation of the European Union (EU) and other regional trading blocs were benefitting large companies able to take advantage of new marketing opportunities in neighboring countries. Sometimes smaller companies got crushed because they lacked the economies of scale compared to their larger competitors.

New business philosophies stressing a broader range of responsibilities added complexities for management for which smaller companies often lacked the expertise to cope. The term "shareholder value" began to be used by executives to explain their new goals and policies. Whatever, in the broadest sense, might enhance the value of the organization for its stakeholders (local communities, shareholders, lenders, workers and so forth) became the responsibility of the CEO.

The people at the top were changing too. Those moving up thru the ranks are being replaced by people from the "outside" who would be less loyal and supportive of internal organization values , but more open to explore new strategies. In fact, often the new leaders came on board with a mandate to lead into uncharted directions. Needless to say conflicts within the executive ranks have intensified.

Gradually American-based multinational companies were feeling the pinch between more stringent environmental laws, higher wages, and benefit costs, as well as increasingly complex and costly tax laws. It is against this backdrop that the theme of this story is developed. Herein, the competing forces are laid bare for all to see. The factual pattern has been repeated many times during the last three decades and has led to an erosion of US economic dominance, but there is now evidence that the pattern has begun to reverse because of increasingly tighter legal requirements imposed by foreign countries.

Despite these trends contributing to the growth of international business, each individual decision is inevitably the result of human decision-making. That process is influenced by personalities, life experiences, sometimes a herd mentality, and the effectiveness of advocates lobbying for particular outcomes.

At the same time, many foreign countries have become active in acquiring new technology through legitimate methods and also through outright theft.

In this story the decision-making process includes the efforts by businesses to adapt to competition, manipulative behavior by greedy executives, espionage by a foreign power, as well as US governmental policy and its defense strategies.

Perhaps, most insightful, this story also reveals the organizational culture that is prevalent in many large businesses. That culture is largely defined by the personal styles and experiences of its leaders.

This author had a front row seat in the course of working for several multinationals and thus had the opportunity to observe how these profound changes played out in the reality.

Hope you enjoy it!

CHAPTER 1

Looking out of the panoramic window from his new office in mid-town Manhattan, Einar Horne, the newly anointed CEO of Specialty Chemicals Incorporated, was in a philosophical mood. "How did I ever end up here?" he asked rhetorically. "One month ago I was ready to hang it up and retire. Hell, we had even narrowed it down to either Cary, North Carolina or maybe somewhere closer to our kids. My somewhat folksy, less pretentious style will be a dramatic change from the previous CEO." It was early March and the first hint of Spring could be seen in Central Park.

He turned and looked at the office that he had inherited and said, "This isn't an office. It's more like a modern art gallery designed to impress visitors about our company's success. It's what my predecessor, Gene Sperling, wanted to feed his ego. I hope it doesn't feed mine too much."

Einar was giving his wife, Sandra, a tour of his new office. "Einar, you complained about that thread-bare office you had in Alabama when you started with this company and now you're still not happy. If this layout doesn't satisfy you, then you've got a real problem."

She's got a point, he thought. I should be happy to have a chance to run this outfit the way that it should be run. If it were not for Gene's missteps, the board's decision about an overseas location and the media speculation about our company's future, I would not be here now. That all led to my promotion, but I need to recognize that it will not sustain me in this job for long.

Meanwhile, down in Anniston, Alabama, the plant employees were aware that they had "dodged a bullet," but were confused as to exactly how that had come about. People were trying to connect the dots and raising frightening questions which nobody seemed to be able to answer. Had there really been a secret nuclear weapons assembly program at their plant? Whatever happened to that Chinese grad student who had interned here and then suddenly disappeared? Did he have anything to do with what's been going on? Were their jobs now secure for the long term or did they have only a temporary reprieve?

The whole series of events that led to the present state of things really started only one year ago. The chronology could be dated from when an eager new hire got unwittingly caught up in company politics, which set in motion the extraordinary events that led to so many unforeseen consequences. These eventualities threatened the livelihood of several hundred plant employees in a town with no other economic options. The rapidly evolving situation also came ominously close to destroying a venerable industrial giant which employed thousands of people. Unknown to most of those involved, a potential threat to the country's national security had also arisen.

* * *

One year earlier, Claire Perkins stood tall and willowy in a nicely tailored gray business suit topped by her freshly styled short brown hair, as she waited for the receptionist to escort her to her new office on this first day of a new beginning. Finally starting a career after so many years of school is one of life's big transitions for someone who basically had never worked for a paycheck.

Two years getting her MBA at the Tuck School of Business at Dartmouth had honed her academic business skills to a razor's edge. Holding her new leather briefcase in her left hand, she graciously extended her right hand to Shirley, who was going to lead her to where Claire would settle into a modest but adequately furnished office.

She reflected on the interview process that led her to this point. Claire had heard horror stories from recently minted "tuckies" (more formally known as graduates from the Amos Tuck business school). Consulting firms were high risk in the opinion of most. Long, long hours, incredible stress, and no job security. Further scouting led her to conclude that a large, well-established company might be a better fit for her as she thought it should be less stressful and would leave time for an outside social life. The downside, of course, could be less opportunity for promotion if the company was no longer expanding, and her new colleagues might be more inbred and resistant to new ideas.

She strode confidently toward the elevator bank while trying to strike up a casual conversation with Shirley, who was at least twice her age and packed a lot of unwanted pounds inside her off-the-rack skirt and blouse.

"So, how do you enjoy working for such a great company?" Claire asked.

"It was interesting in the beginning in 1988, when I started, but now with all of the reorganizations, everyone is on pins and needles."

Wishing to shift to a more neutral subject, Claire said, "At least the weather here in the Big Apple is nice today."

"Sure, but nobody inside the building even notices," Shirley said.

The elevator reached the eighth floor, and as the door slid open, Claire noticed a floor-to-ceiling etched-glass wall that read "Financial Services."

"Which way?" she asked.

Shirley pointed to the left where Claire Perkins saw her name already on the door. After a few words of well wishes, Shirley walked away. Claire slid into the faux leather chair and let her imagination carry her back to the steps that led her to this position.

Graduating from an Ivy League school with honors had meant sacrifices, almost no social life, and giving up her competitive volleyball. Student loans were part of her new reality. Even with a $6,000 per year fellowship, she was keenly aware of the pressure to pay off the $52,000 debt hanging around her neck.

"Hey, girl, don't get too comfy. I have the pleasure of giving you this file, which is now yours to read and make recommendations as to if, and maybe how, we should deal with this project." That was her introduction to Dave who had been with the company a bit over one year. She thought he seemed lacking in confidence and overly cautious despite his kind effort to welcome her.

"Please sit down and talk with me for a few minutes," responded Claire with a wide smile. She was eager to make friends with her new coworkers, particularly those who were near her age and might be able to clue her in to what was really going on.

"Can't right now, but I'll stop by later and maybe we can grab lunch," he said and then disappeared. She began reading the voluminous file he had dropped on her desk.

"Anniston Plant" read the file label. Apparently the company was weighing the costs and benefits of closing the plant and moving the whole operation to a third-world country. Considerations such as environmental laws, taxes, labor union agreements, logistics, and political stability were spelled out in well-reasoned thinking from the legal department, human resources, marketing, property management, and other staff who had weighed in on the project. Claire suspected that she would be asked to analyze all of the available information, possibly request more information, and then prepare a recommendation that incorporated all relevant considerations into a formal proposal to be voted upon by the top brass.

Close the plant and move abroad or not—that was the issue, she decided after thirty minutes of reading. OK, I am certainly academically prepared to make such an analysis and draft a proposal, she confidently assured herself.

At this point she, of course, knew nothing about the plant's operations, its history, the new potential third-world location or the views of senior management. What she did know was that she would attempt to leverage her job for higher visibility, power, and perks, if the situation allowed. Reducing the operations of a $100-million plant to a cash-flow projection would enable the decision-makers to be decisive with plenty of backup data to justify their decision.

Along the way she hoped to meet the key people and impress them with her Ivy League sophistication and knowledge of business analytical skills. At the same time, she did not want to overplay her hand. This was a conservative company run by men a generation older than she.

Meanwhile, six floors higher up, Einar Horne, age sixty-three, with thirty-eight years of company service, gazed vacantly out of his fourteenth-floor Manhattan window toward Central Park. The trees, the lake, and general greenery stretched north some sixty blocks with a view that took his mind briefly away from the hustle-bustle of corporate life.

Einar was still looking out the window when Margie, his former secretary, and now executive assistant, knocked gently on the door frame, and Einar turned toward her.

"Gene is looking for you and likely wants your update on the labor dispute at Anniston."

Gene Sperling, the new CEO, Einar mused.

"I'll bet he does. OK, tell him I'll be there in five minutes." This issue had been on a slow boil for months. Would the company meet demands for better health and dental coverage for union workers or would a strike loom over Anniston?

"Morning, Gene, how was your round on Saturday?" Einar knew his boss would always take time to talk about his golf game and that might defer the serious discussion that he would prefer to avoid.

"I lost three balls on the front nine, and things went downhill from there. Now, Einar, we have got to take a position on this health insurance thing, and you know that plant better than anybody."

"I used to know, but I've been out of there for five years now."

"Maybe, but you still oversee that operation and must have some opinion."

"Gene, it goes like this. First, our realistic cost estimates almost make the federal debt look puny. Second, the union estimates are low, but then they are trying to sell it to us and not having to pay for it. Third, there are so many cross currents, like retirement projections, wage-level forecasts, Obamacare, not to mention whether Anniston should continue to exist, that I honestly don't know what to think."

Gene appreciated Einar's usual candor and replied, "Help has arrived." He then explained that a new financial analyst had just come on board—someone who could help Einar get a grip on the problem. His knowledge of the industry and plant operations coupled with her knowledge of the latest management techniques for working through such a morass should enable a management proposal to be created, which would take into account all of these considerations.

"Einar, her name is Claire Perkins. I'm assigning her to you. She already has the Anniston file. Use her as your gopher to work something up that we can all understand—and do it quickly. I meet with the Board in two weeks, and they will be expecting some recommendations."

Einar left the CEO's office thinking that this new gal, Claire, might be a godsend if, together, they could come up with something that would be fair to everybody and in the best interests of the company. He had the practical company experience, and she would add the latest business-school thinking.

Claire's phone rang. It was Margie telling her that Einar wanted to meet her tomorrow morning to lay out some groundwork for the Anniston project.

Just then Dave, her new colleague, popped his head through the doorway. "Hi, remember me, I'm Dave, the guy who dropped that tome on your desk this morning. How are you settling in?"

"Things seem to be off to a fast start, just the way I like it. I'm supposed to meet with a guy named Einar Horne tomorrow about that project. Who is he really, besides being a VP?"

Dave told her that Einar was rumored to be on the way out, but still knew more about the inner workings of the company than anyone else, and also that he was popular with the rank and file with whom he identified. "Was going to ask you to join me for lunch and meet some of our fellow grunts, but maybe another day."

Claire had finished reading the file and said that meeting some new coworkers would be most welcomed. She wanted to make friends in her new city, get in the loop of inside gossip, and size up any likely competition. Lunch was in the third floor cafeteria. They joined three fellow employees, all about the same age. The conversation quickly focused on Claire because she was brand new to the company.

"Financial Services is the newest department. Our new CEO just organized it about one month ago. He seems to be really interested in shaking this place up," said Aaron, a customer service representative.

"This stogy company could use a good shake," commented Earl, who apparently worked in some aspect of data processing.

That evening, Einar and his wife, Sandra, were unwinding in their apartment off Fifth Avenue. "You know, Sandy, I'm earning more than ever before, but the satisfaction is just not there anymore."

"Einar, I think I've heard this before. We should have stayed in Alabama and rode it out till retirement, but we are here now, and there's no going back."

Einar and Sandra had been married for thirty-six years and could often read each other's thoughts. He had gone to work for one of the nation's top chemical companies without any particular thought of moving up the corporate ladder, but that advancement had come to him because he had the practical know-how and people skills to get things done in a manufacturing environment.

Sandra had started a teaching career but after several years had found a loving partner in Einar. Then the two children had come in rapid succession, and she never went back to the classroom.

She knew that it helped her husband to relax if she listened politely when he was in one of these moods, even if it had become repetitive over the past several years.

"These guys I work with now could not begin to run a production facility, but that's key to our business, and they're making decisions about stuff they don't understand," he said.

Sandra listened patiently.

"I guess I'm really like them in that I don't appreciate assessing investor reactions or legal risks, and yet I am now dealing with that kind of stuff every day. Maybe this means our company's decisions are being made by people who don't comprehend what they're doing. It's a wonder that the company stayed in business for so many years," Einar said as he poured another glass of wine.

"My strength is that I know the nuts and bolts of getting consistent product out the door, but that doesn't count for much with these headquarters executives and their staffs. These guys thrive on controversy and hide behind the vagaries of unclear laws and unpredictable outside forces."

"Well, if you feel that way, maybe it's time to retire," Sandra said.

"I've got to hang on a little longer because I'm the only one who stands between these headquarters guys and the rank and file employees who do the real work. Tomorrow, though, should be fun. Gene's assigned me a new business analyst to help develop recommendations for Anniston. We meet first thing in the morning."

The next day, Einar welcomed Claire into his tastefully decorated office and asked her about her upbringing in the leafy Boston suburb of Natick, her business studies at Dartmouth, and how she was settling into life in the Big Apple. Claire smoothly gave answers that she knew would create a favorable impression on a man of Einar's background. Then she asked him about his background just as her business psychology professor had taught her to do.

"I'm the old guard," he replied. "Engineering degree from Purdue. In my career I mainly learned how to get consistent product out the factory door at a reasonable cost."

These were good insights, which would help her deal with him. She felt instinctively that she could manipulate him through her knowledge of modern business theories about which he probably knew little. Best to draw him out, she thought, as she said, "Those must have been interesting times, being involved in how the company grew to over a billion dollars in annual sales."

"Looking back, I would not trade those experiences for the world," he replied with a nostalgic smile. "Great friendships, building a solid organization, meeting customer needs, and getting a sense of accomplishment, that's what it's all about

"That file you bought in here titled Anniston is your first assignment," he told her. "That operation has become rather controversial, because it's an old plant, with strong union representation, and now questions about its costs are beginning to surface."

She sat up straighter, knowing this was going to be a big assignment. Her first.

"Claire, first I want you to go to the plant and talk to all the key people, get a sense of how things are really going, not just financial numbers and production figures, and, for God's sake, don't say anything about any wild ideas to move the plant abroad. If it comes up, just say you don't know anything about it. Stay away from the union people and then relate what you learned in a project report that our staffers here put together and then we'll talk. See you in about a week."

Wow, thought Claire, my second day on the job and I'm off on a business trip! What's behind this? Her next thought was what to wear to visit a plant in Alabama, considering she'd never even visited a factory in her life and never been south of the Mason-Dixon line.

After she left his office, Einar thought, getting her to meet some plant employees, seeing how things work at that level, should be a good way to teach her about realities before she did any business theory analysis. She's just starting out and has no feel for what it takes to run an operation like this. Being able to quantify everything down to a gnat's eyelash and then making a decision is probably how she will approach this Anniston situation. Hopefully, I can adjust her mindset just enough to factor in some informed intuition.

Claire could already see the potential for her success at the company. She had already had access to a senior executive. Gleaning the maximum amount of relevant information in Anniston and deciding who favors what outcome would be her next priority.

CHAPTER 2

"Your first visit to Anniston, Ms. Perkins?" Jimmy liked picking up plant visitors and driving them around. He was almost as proud of his fourteen years at the company as he was singing in the men's choir at AME Baptist.

Claire replied, "Oh yes, in fact, this is my first visit to Alabama. I'm a Yankee, born and raised."

"Thought I detected a foreign accent on you. Likely this heat will take some getting used to."

The van approached the main gate, and Claire could see the large dusty parking lot mainly inhabited by pickup trucks, a few motorcycles, and a variety of older, smaller cars. A large sign read, "No accidents for 220 days."

Jimmy parked and took her inside to meet the plant manager, Bill Vaalens. The affable, rotund Bill rose from his desk and said with a big smile, "Well, well, we don't often get visitors as pretty as you, Ms. Perkins. Welcome to the country's best industrial chemicals plant."

Bill, or Billy as his friends called him, often felt left out when it came to changes in company policy, typically receiving new directives that he sometimes didn't agree with, but was expected to implement. He saw in Claire's visit a chance to get some corporate inside scoop, impress her with the plant's efficiency, and maybe learn something more of a personal nature.

Claire's impression at this point was that she had entered a world that could best be described as "red neck central" and that she would really need to figure out how to communicate with these people if she was to succeed here.

Meanwhile, back in another world, on the fourteenth floor at company headquarters in New York, the operations committee was settling around their gigantic redwood table with water glasses and note pads placed in front of each seat. Gene swept in last, as was his style, and promptly called the meeting to order.

Agendas sat in front of each attendee. The packets were smaller than usual with only three items to be discussed.

The first item on the agenda was Anniston. Second, renewing an advertising campaign for chemical intermediates, and last, a progress report on efforts to clean up a waste dump site from the 1960s, which was now under the watchful eye of the federal EPA.

"Let's take them in reverse order," said Gene, asserting his leadership. "So, Einar, what's the latest with the site cleanup."

Einar tried to speak in carefully measured sentences. He explained that the site was used to dump chemical waste before America even had environmental laws, and now the seepage had gone into the groundwater, and there was no way to clean it up. They all knew this from earlier reports, but also knew that something, some type of progress, must be reported for both PR purposes and to avoid further EPA and state fines.

"We could put filters at the thirty-odd places where the groundwater flowed to municipal utilities and in the aquifers used by farmers, but the cost would be at least sixty million dollars and with no guarantee that the problem would be completely resolved," concluded Einar.

The other committee members had no questions or comments because they lacked the expertise in this area and had heard this story more than a few times. Quite often those who made it to the upper ranks of corporate America were highly competent in a specific business area and also had the emotional intelligence to develop rapport with their colleagues. However, when it came to areas outside of their expertise, they often were indecisive for fear of later criticism.

"Nothing new," said Gene after a long pause and then told them that the board expected some decision from them. "I'll tell them sixty million dollars, with a better than fifty-fifty chance of ending this issue." They all knew that $60 million would put the fiscal year in a loss position. Bye-bye bonuses. Quite often those who made it to the upper ranks of corporate America were also cautious about taking positions on key issues.

Don Osborn, the vice president of public relations and advertising, now took the floor to discuss his budget—the second item on the agenda. He was a kindred spirit of Gene's in the sense that they had similar professional backgrounds having both had experience in advertising firms. "I don't see much sales bang for the buck putting our money into these trade shows and industry publications. Our products are not purchased by consumers. These types of advertisements don't persuade purchasing agents to buy our products. They look to technical specifications, warranties, and our level of technical backup in making purchasing decisions. I would like to put more money into promoting our technical support function."

"How much money?" asked Gene from the head of the table.

"Half of my twenty-two-million-dollar budget," responded Don. He was eventually asked to come back next month with some hard numbers explaining specifically how the technical support function could best be promoted and at what cost. Everyone agreed that if the customers believed that the tech support was high quality and responsive, then sales would increase.

Anniston had been a burr under the saddle for several years, and the problems just seemed to pile up. Einar rose again to speak about the issues in the Alabama plant.

"We've got a new hotshot MBA down there now. She and I will put our heads together next week and make some concrete recommendations," said Einar.

Gene nodded and then said, "We will meet here in two weeks to hear your recommendations, Einar." The pressure was being ratcheted up.

Some years back when Einar was running the plant in Alabama, it manufactured a highly toxic nerve gas called VX for the US Army and won plaudits by doing so without any injuries or mishaps. The remaining stockpile of this nerve gas had now finally been destroyed in accordance with a Soviet-American treaty. The residue had been buried on the plant grounds in concrete pipes with the ends sealed with stainless steel caps. Only two people at the plant knew the real story, and only one was still alive.

Now a different, highly classified product was being produced in miniscule quantities. No one locally knew its intended use, only that once a month a small truck with US Air Force markings would take delivery.

Meanwhile down south, Claire was busy absorbing information. She had interviewed everyone that she could find who had working knowledge of the plant. She was reviewing her notes with Billy, who was amused by her questions because they revealed a complete lack of manufacturing knowledge and a naiveté about blue-collar factory workers.

"Einar called to say that you need to get back to headquarters tomorrow because the brass has moved up the deadline for your report. Guess you won't have time to see 'Bama in action this Saturday against LSU."

Billy was a big fish in a little pond, but realized that Claire was not impressed with him in the way he had hoped.

"Just one more thing," she said. "I have not really toured all of the real estate here and want to get a feel for the size and what borders the plant grounds."

"OK, we'll make that your last look."

Jimmy was called in and told to take her around the perimeter of the two hundred acres that the company owned and then drive her to the airport for an evening flight. Nearly a third of the grounds were not used, and a swampy area prevented passage by vehicle to over twenty acres. The land surrounding the plant had been built up over the years with low-income housing on one side and a wildlife refuge adjacent to the swamp.

"What goes on there?" Claire asked, pointing to a small barn-like structure separated from the rest of the plant.

"That's an air force operation. We don't know exactly what they do, and it's off-limits to all regular employees," replied Jimmy.

Claire made a note to ask about it later.

Upon her return to corporate headquarters after a five-day visit to the Alabama plant, she felt that she now better understood the competing forces that were vying to win the issue of whether to close the plant, keep it open, or perhaps reduce the operations.

"So, how did the 'Bama boys treat you down there, Ms. Perkins?" Einar wanted to hear all about her trip, particularly the mood of the employees in view of all the issues on the table: the union push for more health care coverage, the rumors about closing and moving offshore to save costs, and whether she had picked up any rumors about toxic material storage concerns.

"The boys treated me like royalty," she declared with a broad smile.

"That's as expected. Now give me your thoughts about what we might put in a recommendation to our board."

Claire responded by saying that she had not yet evaluated how the plant fits in with the new corporate vision for the future of the company overall.

"Come on now, you must have formed some opinions. Why do you think we sent you down there?"

"OK, the plant is old. The EPA is strangling us with tighter and tighter rules, and it doesn't seem to have many positives for our shareholders going forward." She had not wanted to be drawn out at such an early point, but he had forced it out of her. So she added, "But that's just a preliminary impression, of course."

To shift the direction of the conversation, she then asked him, "What's the deal with that air force operation, separate from everything else?"

"Actually, I know very little about it. It was never under my management of Anniston. We simply provide a building on company land and the Air Force pays the rent. We were happy to lease the space and not have any further responsibility for what they were doing."

Einar smiled, but more to cover up his disappointment. "There are many unknowns, particularly those associated with moving the operation overseas. How would the shareholders really benefit in the long run? That's what we have to figure out. Strategic vision cannot so easily be reduced to numbers, and so it takes a sort of horse sense to come to the right decision."

Claire replied, "Perhaps, but most of the unknowns can be quantified within a predictable range, and that will give us some backup if we are challenged."

"We, for sure, will be challenged, and the buzzards are circling already," said Einar.

Claire wanted to know where the other decision-makers stood on these issues before she prepared a more formal report, but how to do that? She could try to make friends with those who worked closely with the other senior executives, but that would take more time than she had. Gaining access and then charming them into revealing their opinions might not work because most would probably wait until a formal recommendation was presented and then see who lined up on which side of the issue before taking a position.

At least that's the way her professors had told her that most such decisions are actually made.

She felt that she personally had no stake in the ultimate outcome, so she focused mainly on how she could come off looking good in the eyes of those who could influence her progress in the company.

CHAPTER 3

CLAIRE ARRIVED FIVE minutes early for her appointment with Gene Sperling, the most senior company executive. He had summoned her to get acquainted and also to get a sense of what new information she may have uncovered in Alabama. Looking around the sumptuous reception area, she could feel the wealth that radiated from the collection of exotic Asian art that faced her from the opposite wall. The expansive view behind her showcased the downtown skyline.

"You must be Claire, I'm Gene, the guy who can't pass the buck to anyone else around here. Please come in." Gene led her into the largest single office that she had ever seen. An eclectic mix of furnishings met her eyes. A stone fireplace stood in the middle of the room with a Scandinavian-style teak desk accented with polished chrome. Behind the desk and on the walls were pictures of Gene posing with well-known celebrities and politicians.

"Let's sit over here," Gene said as he motioned toward a large contemporary sofa. "So tell me, after, what, one week on the job, is it, what do you think about our little company?"

"Love it," she replied with a broad smile.

"Nice to hear that, but now tell me what you learned down there in good old Alabamy. And how does it square with what you've heard up here?"

Claire had anticipated such a question and gave her well-thought-out reply. "Things up here are not in sharp focus because there are too many unresolved issues, and the boys in Alabama are too narrowly concerned with what's best for them."

Gene laughed and said, "I have no doubt that accurately sums it up, but we have to make a concrete recommendation to the board about what to do with Anniston."

Just then Gene's executive assistant, Sarah, entered and said, "Are you aware that there are two investment bankers patiently waiting for you?" Both Gene and Claire arose and he said, "We'll take this up later, say, how about dinner tomorrow night, away from all of this corporate culture?"

Claire was stunned, but smiled and said, "That would be great!"

"I'll let you know where and at what time," and with that he was gone.

Wow, did I score or what, she mused to herself. What an opportunity. She would need a new dress, something business appropriate, but also feminine.

The Four Seasons is a restaurant designed to impress. "Did you have any trouble finding the place?" Gene asked casually. After the dinner and wine were ordered, he asked, "How were we able to attract someone like you to Manhattan and away from that rustic New England countryside?"

"It was easy actually. I wanted a change of scenery and an opportunity to see what I can really achieve." She was now recognizing that Gene was a suave, well-groomed, polished man who matched her long-held fantasy. She began to feel a bit giddy.

Gene could sense her reaction and decided to keep the conversation on a personal level rather than asking questions about her work project. He asked, "So, what did you do on those long cold winters in New Hampshire?"

"There were only two, and I studied indoors most of the time and only took a break for the Winter Carnival in Hanover in midwinter. It's an annual winter sports and partying event at Dartmouth that helps us get through those long winters."

"Life in Manhattan must be quite a change," Gene responded.

She replied that so far she had barely begun to explore the city, but was looking forward to learning her way around.

After their second glass of wine, they were both relaxing in their secluded corner table enjoying the soft background music when a distinguished white-haired man broke the mood by stepping forward.

"Gene, I thought it was you. Don't want to bother you now, but we should get together to review the new ad campaign."

"I'll call you, Harry, and we'll set it up," Gene said curtly.

Harry moved off realizing that his intrusion had not been welcomed. Claire could see that this swanky restaurant was one that Gene's colleagues patronized.

"Harry and I go way back. We wrote advertising copy together, not five blocks from here," Gene said. "You see, Claire, my perspective is that the most important aspects of business are not mere differences of fact, but customer perception, image, and the more subliminal dimensions. That's why the board hired me, to build a new image of the company that would translate into higher stock valuations."

She said she knew he had come up from a public relations/advertising background. This also gave her a clue as to how to handle him. Skip the numbers and focus on the softer side of business.

"You, for example, will enhance our image as a company, by showing that we are not just a bunch of over-the-hill stodgy old men. We need a fresher image, and you can help with that."

"Being part of the fresher image would be fun," she responded with a grin.

He then complimented her dress and style, saying, "We could form a powerful partnership and revitalize the corporate image."

Claire saw her opening and smiled seductively saying, "A partnership out of the office would be good too."

Gene paused and said, "I'm in the midst of a messy divorce and feeling very lonely now." He gazed at her. His ruggedly handsome tanned face combined with those blue eyes was mesmerizing. Claire felt the power of his charming demeanor.

Both saw that a personal connection was a distinct possibility, but Claire was now nervous thinking she had overstepped her position. She took the conversation in a different direction by noting the time and saying, "This has really been a great evening but it's way past the bed time for a working gal who has to be sharp at an uncivilized early hour tomorrow." Claire hailed a cab to her tiny eastside apartment.

A seed was laid for the future with both realizing the risks and potential benefits that might lie ahead. Gene realized the effect that he had on young women when he turned on the charm. It was likely, he thought, that Claire would try to please him and that she could be expected to support his ideas for the company.

Claire realized that maybe she was in over her head. Meeting the CEO for dinner was a high-stakes proposition from her viewpoint, but if she made a good impression, it was worth the effort. Now that effort had led to a veiled invitation to something more personal, and she was afraid. Better be more cautious around him, she concluded.

The next day Einar was meeting with Jim Johnson, a site selection specialist in the corporate real estate division. Jim had just returned from an Asian swing. A seasoned veteran with the company, he knew how to evaluate the pros and cons of where manufacturing operations could flourish and could also see the red flags. He always tried to tell it like he saw it.

Einar knew and trusted his judgment. "So where in the world would be better than Anniston?" he asked Jim.

"Einar, Asia is slowly becoming less attractive generally because of the development of those laws, cultural sensitivities, infrastructure problems, and unions that drove US industry to move south after World War II. I don't believe we gain much of anything going to a third-world country."

Einar smiled and said, "That was what I thought you would tell me."

"Yes, but I said generally, however, because each country that I looked at was somewhat different. What is the same is that we need to give weight to our customers' need for quick, reliable deliveries, technical support, and financing, which would seem to give a big edge to staying in the USA. Wage savings are there, but with our products, labor content is minimal. It's not like a labor-intensive product where assembly and packaging make up most of the product cost like, say, clothing."

Einar was really beginning to appreciate this guy. "Yes, meeting customer needs must come first," he said with conviction. They both looked up to see Claire standing in the doorway. "Come in and meet Jim."

After introductions, Jim asked them to keep his opinions confidential for a while, recognizing that he had just given too much inside information in front of Claire, who was new to the organization. Jim left leaving Claire and Einar looking at each other.

"His thoughts are very preliminary, and he said he needs to refine the data before getting together with us," Einar said.

Claire felt insulted and told Einar, "Look, I'm supposed to be getting all the information on this project. What gives?"

Einar blushed and simply replied, "Be patient. Jim just dropped by. There is no intention to keep you out of the loop. Quite the contrary."

She knew she must assert herself to be taken seriously; otherwise, she might be perceived as an overeducated clerk, but standing up for herself too brashly could backfire. Probably I just came across as some kind of control freak, she thought.

Just as I suspected, he's making a case to protect his buddies in Alabama and probably thinks I favor the relocation to Asia, thought Claire. Trust between them was rapidly evaporating. She would have to do something to restore it. Einar was, after all, her boss.

CHAPTER 4

LOOKING OUT THE tiny window of her office, Claire could see the weather was turning nasty. This would be her first free weekend in the city, and she was looking forward to it, rain or shine. Her younger coworkers had mentioned the "edgier" clubs in Soho and the bars on the Upper East Side.

"Dave," she called from her desk as she saw her male cohort walk by. He stopped and popped his head inside her doorway.

"You called, my lady," he said with a smile. She then said that if he were looking for fun, either tonight or tomorrow night, maybe he could show her around.

"Got a hot date tonight, but Saturday night could work," he replied. They made arrangements to meet at a popular bar near her apartment in the Upper East 70s at nine o'clock and then drop in on some of these "in" spots.

Claire was not interested in Dave on a personal level, but he would be a good escort for her first evening on the town. He was too short for her five-foot eight-inch frame, but she felt secure being with him. .

Saturday night came, and she saw Dave waiting at the bar. He bought her a drink. Claire chose a light beer, after deciding to pace herself through the next three or four hours.

The next stop was highly recommended by Dave. She stepped inside and could smell the marijuana wafting through the air. He merely said this was the kind of place where you could let your hair down. Soon she was puffing the magic dragon that he offered to her. Her inhibitions began to loosen, and soon she was dancing under the strobe lights with a guy she had not even met. That was her last memory of the evening.

As the morning light gradually gazed upon her face, Claire asked no one in particular, "Where am I?" Her head was throbbing, and she knew she was not in a familiar place. She had fallen asleep on a rather worn sofa in her black party dress.

"You're in Brooklyn, sweetheart. Brighton Beach to be more exact," came the foreign-accented reply. She looked around in alarm and saw that she was in a shabby apartment with two other people. Several posters worded in Cyrillic script decorated the walls. A large silver colored samovar seemed to be the only piece of décor worth noting. A small sofa was the only piece of furniture that looked reasonably new.

"I'm Natasha and this is Alex," said a slender blonde of approximately her same age. "We brought you to our place by cab after you passed out while dancing with Alex. This coffee should help clear your head."

"What about Dave?" Claire asked.

"We don't know Dave," they both replied with a shrug.

After a long shower, at Natasha's suggestion, and several cups of coffee, Claire left her new friends and managed to navigate the subway system to her home early Sunday afternoon. Despite not fully knowing how she had ended up in Brooklyn, Claire thought the evening had been exciting..

Later that day, the phone rang, and Natasha asked if she got home OK.

"I'm going to bed until I need to go to work tomorrow morning," Claire said.

"Don't forget our party this coming Friday night. I'll send you directions by e-mail."

Monday morning left Claire still wondering what had really happened. She must talk with Dave and find out. Dave's recall was rather sketchy. He lost track of her and eventually went home and fell asleep.

The evening had been exciting after so many study nights in New Hampshire. She wanted more, but knew that she must not let things get out of control. The coming party on Friday night in Brighton Beach should be exciting. Her new Russian friends had taken care of her and she now trusted them. This was what she had hoped the nightlife would be all about. Her desire for some fun grew over the workdays, so by Friday she was ready to party. She found that being with people from a different part of the world was stimulating and they had already come to her aid.

She struggled through the workweek without any particular enthusiasm. Now it was Friday afternoon. She went home and prepared for the party with these new friends.

Brighton Beach is now a predominantly Russian community near Coney Island in Brooklyn. Claire climbed the stairs to Alex's second-floor walk-up apartment. She felt safe. After all, it was these people who had taken her to their home and allowed her to sleep safely, freshen up and explained how to travel back to her apartment on the subway.

Loud music pulsated from the apartment. The door was wide open, and the small apartment was crowded with people speaking what Claire assumed was Russian.

A tall blond guy with a big grin approached her. "You must be Claire. I'm Natasha's brother, Oleg." He handed her a drink of some sort, which tasted strongly of vodka. An hour later the room seemed to be spinning. She slid on to the familiar sofa she had slept on a week ago and soon was falling unconscious.

This time she woke up in her own bed with Oleg lying beside her. He grinned at her and then said in a mocking tone that "she was special and they should do it again soon."

Despite a pounding headache, Claire stood up and ordered Oleg to get dressed and leave immediately. With a smirk, he slowly complied.

Claire had never faced such a situation in her life. She trembled with rage, but did not explode with anger because she was more scared than angry. After Oleg left, she showered and began to reflect on her life and how she had gotten to this point.

Growing up in a pleasant Boston suburb, such as Natick, did not ensure a happy childhood. Claire's mother, Anne, had been an alcoholic. When Anne fell down the stairs and broke her hip, the family lost an important source of income.

Her dad had a habit of squandering money on gambling, so nearly every month, the family barely squeaked by. Claire was determined not to repeat this dysfunctional pattern. Her resolve motivated her to excel at school.

Her one brother, Arne, had gone the other way. Drugs and criminal behavior were his way of coping. He had tried to enlist in the marines, the navy, and finally the air force, but they had all turned him down because of his use of illegal drugs. All of these rejections had led him to begin group therapy, with Claire's strong encouragement.

Finally he saw an avenue for success by enrolling in a new local community college program to become certified in medical device repairs. Unfortunately his old drug habits continued to jeopardize his future, but Claire counterbalanced with money and encouragement.

Claire felt obliged to help Arne, but with her now living in New York, and him in the Boston area, her support consisted of monthly cash infusions, which she suspected were sometimes converted to bodily infusions.

A few weeks later Gene Sperling, happened to catch the same elevator as Claire, but he only nodded to acknowledge her presence. Was this his way of saying that the "more personal relationship" that seemed possible a short while ago was now not going to happen?

"I'll bet it's a wig," whispered Martha to her coworker in the employee cafeteria as Gene passed by on his way to the executive dining room.

Alice said, "You're probably right. No man fifty-eight years old could look that great naturally."

Salt-and-pepper hair, perfectly trimmed, sat on top of that confident smile, which projected exactly what he wanted to convey.

Indeed Gene took incredible pride in his image and appearance. Tall, lean, toned and tanned, he was resplendent in his custom-tailored suit and designer tie. Bob, a new intern, also saw Gene pass through the cafeteria and wondered if he might ever reach such heights in his business career.

Gene mused as he strode across the room, Look at them, the women yearning to reach me and the men idolizing me for my success. This was a payoff that stroked his ego.

Gene lived by the philosophy that image and perception trumped hard facts and could overcome almost any obstacle. Clearly, he was the success story of that philosophy. Coming into the business world from The Harvard Business School, he had started with a large advertising company. Showing his creative streak, determination, and people skills, and with a little luck, Gene moved up the ladder and was creative director by age forty-six, but he was growing restless to move into a top corporate position.

His chance came twelve years later when an old-line chemical manufacturer, named Chemical Specialties, with an image problem, was trying to reposition itself in a rapidly changing marketplace. Their top management realized that new blood was needed to take the reins, which had begun to slip from their hands. This move eventually led to Gene taking over as CEO.

Twice divorced and looking for someone to complement his "prominent position" and convey an appearance of a secure, well-settled family man, Gene was using an exclusive dating service to deliver candidates who would fit the profile.

With his first board meeting behind him, Gene now focused on his upcoming date.

"Well, book her on the flight tonight and put her up in the Plaza Hotel, and I'll wine and dine her tomorrow night. I'm reserving the evening, so make it happen." Gene was easily angered if the dating service was unable to deliver as if the "goods" were some commodity.

"OK, Gene, we'll get her there, and we want you to know that our vetting has been completed and she checks out very well."

Marsha Soper was used to dealing with demanding clients. Having developed this high-end business from scratch some fifteen years earlier, Marsha knew that Gene would like Sonja because she fit the profile that they had carefully crafted. The problem could be that Sonja might not like him.

Marsha called Sonja to confirm the details.

"Sonja, it's all set up. Just get up here. There will be a ticket in your name at Miami International Airport for a 9:20am flight tomorrow to JFK," said Marsha.

"I'm already packed, so it should work," whispered Sonja into her cell phone.

The Palm Room is a high-end watering hole on the ground floor of the Plaza Hotel on Central Park South. It caters mostly to out-of-town business executives. The next day at 6:00 p.m. most unoccupied heads turned to enjoy the visual feast of a gorgeous thirty-something woman striding across the floor toward an equally attractive man in his mid-fifties.

"Gene, it's a pleasure and thanks for the invitation to visit New York," gushed Sonja. They shook hands and sat down while the gawkers resumed their previous activities.

An elusive "chemistry" seemed to roll over the couple like an invisible fog. She had the look that Gene was seeking. Confident, with an air of elegance and style. She seemed to rise above her surroundings. Sonja also was impressed with Gene and her New York surroundings. She wondered if he would be the key to a lifestyle to which she had long aspired.

CHAPTER 5

This is the most depressing time, probably because everyone else is so cheerful, thought Claire.

Yes, the Christmas spirit had even permeated corporate headquarters. Seasonal music, candy canes, wreaths on office doors, and even Santa was expected this afternoon to hear the wishes of the staff members. No office party was scheduled because the staff lived at all points of the compass, some north in Tarrytown, some east on Long Island, and others in New Jersey.

Few knew about Claire's family background, only that she was from suburban Boston. She thought about going home to Natick, but with her parents now deceased and her only brother, Arne, in jail for possession and intention to distribute, Natick did not seem the place to be during the holidays.

"Hi, Claire, guess you'll be heading up north for Christmas," said Dave.

"Not this year," she replied vaguely. Claire had no plans yet, but going up to Natick would definitely not be under consideration.

"Say, maybe you would like to come down to Broome Street and help out with the homeless. I did it last year, and it was very satisfying."

"Doing what?" she replied without much enthusiasm.

"Several things. Give out warm clothes, clean up the hall, and dish out food contributed by city restaurants."

Claire nodded that she heard him, but thought it would not be her idea for a merry holiday. Christmas Eve was tomorrow, and she had procrastinated by not making any plans, and now it was too late to book anything. Tomorrow I'll sleep in and then go for a spa day she decided. The pampering consisted of a whirlpool bath, massage, nails, facial, and finally an elegant hairstyle. This will be my own Christmas present to myself, she decided. By luck, she got an appointment when someone else canceled at the last minute.

It was four in the afternoon on Christmas Eve, and the winter sky was already beginning to grow dark. A cold, damp wind was blowing, and the slush on the streets had not fully melted. She stepped from Elizabeth Arden's Fifth Avenue salon feeling reborn, when a darting yellow cab zoomed by and sprayed dirty street water over her new hairdo and facial.

Claire was transfixed for a moment, but her anger soon passed when she realized how superficial and vain she was becoming. Now I'm too big of a mess to go anyplace but back to my apartment, which was a dismal thought. Just as she was beginning to trudge up Fifth Avenue toward her apartment building, a small sign on the railing of a subway entrance caught her eye. "Help those who need it most. Shared holidays are better."

"I'll do it," she said aloud to no one in particular. Several minutes later, after a brief study of the subway map, she was on her way to the Lower East Side and hoped that she remembered the street where Dave had said he volunteered.

Upon exiting the subway to the street, it was now dark and she felt uncomfortable in such a run-down neighborhood. She would need to ask for directions to Broome Street, thanking God that she had at least remembered that street name. An elderly black man with a bent back shuttled toward her, as she called out, "Looking for Broome Street, do you know it?"

"Sure I knows it. It's where I'm a'heading. Wouldn't walk around here if I didn't know where I was going," he replied, looking her up and down. "I got a washcloth in my pocket if you want to wipe that dirt off you."

Embarrassed, she quickly wiped at her face and hair in the near darkness until he said she looked good.

Ten minutes later, she was approaching a busy place, with lots of down and out people hanging around. This must be the place, Claire thought. Dave will be surprised to see me.

Already feeling slightly better about her situation, she entered the crowded hall and asked for Dave.

"Dave Hainesworth, you mean?"

"Yes."

"Well he's gone now. What can I do for you?"

"I want to help out," she replied without forethought.

"Need some help with the pots and pans tonight. Can you do that?" Her expensive clothes and dirty face mystified the man she was speaking to. "Go to the back and tell Mabel that you're here to help her," said the man who had not introduced himself.

Claire trotted off to the dishwashing area without further conversation.

Scrubbing pots soon destroyed her fresh manicure, and there was now soapy water on her designer sweater. Finally, Mabel said, "Take a break, hun."

Claire walked into the crowded, dirty ladies room and surveyed herself. What a mess. After another hour she was told to go home and celebrate the Lord's birthday.

Two days later, after the holiday, and a three-day weekend, Dave walked into her office with a smile and said, "I really didn't expect that you would show up down there."

"It surprised me too," she said.

Christmas had gone from a self-inflicted downer to a collective celebration. It dawned on Claire that she had actually done charitable work for the first time in her memory. The sense of satisfaction was beginning to break down her self-centeredness. At work too, for the first time, she was beginning to identify with team goals and results.

CHAPTER 6

On the other side of the world, the company's CEO was just arriving for his first visit to the Far East.

So far, so good, thought Gene Sperling, seated in first class, as his commercial flight glided to a smooth landing at Hong Kong's busy international airport, which had replaced the earlier one situated on landfill near the heart of downtown. Here he had arranged a two-day recuperative holiday, followed by several business briefings about manufacturing in Asia.

The drive to the Peninsula Hotel was in the luxury tradition that had existed since long before Britain surrendered the colony to the People's Republic. All registered guests are delivered in a Rolls Royce from the airport to the hotel. Gene felt rested after sleeping in his fully reclining first-class seat for most of his long flight. He was ready for a shower, change of clothes, and then some sightseeing.

He did not notice that he was being observed by a squat round man with a pockmarked face who sat in the lobby reading a Chinese language newspaper.

"He's checking in now," the man communicated to his cell phone and then resumed reading the paper.

Gene had traveled by himself to Hong Kong for a particular reason. He alone would receive the briefings and ask questions. That would give him the flexibility to frame his trip reports with information that would convey his personal views to the board without any fear of being challenged.

An hour later, Gene walked to the Victoria Peak cable car, but decided not to go up because he could see the fog rolling in, which would make impossible any observation of the city from the top of Hong Kong's highest point. While pondering what to do next, a cab driver approached Gene with an offer to visit a gentlemen's club. Gene decided to go and savor the lovelies of Asia, as his driver was describing them.

The club was a garishly lit modern building with a large neon red dragon over the door.

"I'm Suzy and I am going to show you a good time," said a slender Asian woman in a bright green dress. She took Gene by the arm and seated him in a booth near the ongoing floor show of a traditional Chinese morality play. Such plays are typically short, colorful and with simple direct messages about family virtues.

"You are a handsome American man, I know from your clothes," she said. Gene responded with an offer to buy both of them a drink.

He asked her where she lived, and she replied that all the club girls lived in Repulse Bay, which Gene had heard was the most expensive residential area in Hong Kong. He learned that she was a college graduate and fluent in Mandarin, Cantonese, and English.

"I am here for five days and could use a good guide," he said. "Any chance that I could hire you to show me around?"

"You pay me more than I make here for the same time, and I'm your girl," she replied without hesitation. Gene thought he was really going to enjoy this visit with her showing him around.

The next day, Suzy began her duties as Gene's guide. She displayed an amazing grasp of the area, not only tourist spots but also about the business culture, which was nearly incomprehensible to Gene. He asked her to continue working for him during the business phase of his visit. She took the business meetings in stride, often asking questions on her own initiative in both Chinese and English.

At the end of his visit to Hong Kong, Gene invited Suzy to apply for a new position at the company as Asian resource manager, which he had just created.

They took the Star Ferry to Kowloon and then went to Guangzhou on the bullet train to evaluate available factory space, labor costs, legal formalities, and related matters. Again, Suzy proved to be invaluable, and they compiled detailed information in only three days, which would allow Gene to prepare a positive report that he thought could justify the move from Alabama to China.

Suzy excused herself to make a cell phone call. A squat man with a pockmarked face answered. She said, "He bought it, hook, line, and sinker. I'll be back tonight. He's flying back to New York tomorrow, thinks he has all the information he needs to sell his board on the move to China."

Gene was so enthusiastic about the information collected that he began writing his report during the long flight back to New York. Labor costs would be 30 percent less than in the United States, with no benefits necessary, and taxes would be lower than in Alabama. It was a no-brainer!

Two weeks later, Gene's recent visit to China was now on the agenda of a government policy meeting taking place in Beijing.

Lu Bow, a Politburo member and economist, expressed his view of how the national export earnings decline could be offset. The unrealistically low foreign exchange value of the Chinese currency had, of course, stimulated export sales, but the government wanted more.

"Yes, get them, particularly the Americans, to invest here," he told the policymakers. "Their capital can build our job base. With the flow of peasants coming into the cities, we must have paid employment for them, or we will invite social unrest. Remember, since the time that our economy has been liberated, our annual per capita growth rate has exceeded nine percent from 1990 through 2012. This rate has never been exceeded in history."

Shu Mae Li, from the finance ministry, responded, "The foreigners will then own the production assets whether they are factory assets, trucks, or whatever. Do we want that?"

"Perhaps not, but we control the legal structure and can impose taxes and, thereby, effectively use their capital to further our political objectives," said Lu Bow. "Once they invest, it will gradually be more and more difficult for them to repatriate cash or other assets. Chinese law prohibits anyone, even Chinese citizens, from removing assets from the country without government approval. Remember, too, Americans have no loyalty to their own country, only to their profits, so we must convince them that their profitability will be greater by investing in China than elsewhere.

Shu Mae Li interrupted what was now becoming a lecture by pointing out her own role in all of this. "We can do that by leading them to information that will support their decisions to invest here."

Lu Bow, somewhat incensed at the interruption, continued "Our Ministry of Economics will be critical in providing statistics that will lead foreigners to the inevitable conclusion that China is the best place to invest. Capital flows to where it is expected to get the best rate of return. I learned that at the University of Chicago ten years ago."

After a pause to digest this information, Shu Mae Li asked, "If we are successful in getting all of this foreign investment, won't our currency strengthen, raising labor costs and making our exports less competitive?"

"Of course, over the very long term that will happen, but then we will do the buying of Western assets in the US and elsewhere and thus gain a firm foothold in their economies," replied Lu Bow, with a self-satisfied grin..

He continued, "Now most of the individual US states are competing against each other for investments that will create jobs. By offering tax holidays and training subsidies, we can demonstrate lower wages, looser environmental laws, and cheaper energy costs than almost anywhere. We must acknowledge, at least among ourselves, that often being far from the customers increases delivery and insurance costs, but we can even minimize these negatives. We have state-owned shipping companies that are very competitive and can ship around the world at lower costs than some private shipping companies."

Assistant business development specialist Ne Xing pointed out that a large American-based multinational company was considering closing a plant in the American South and moving their production to China.

"We have intelligence agents posing as commercial real estate agents, tour guides, and Chamber of Commerce people who are doing their patriotic duty to influence the decision to move here. We sometimes exaggerate our advantages, but the foreigners seem to take what they hear at face value. A CEO named Gene Sperling is a key decision-maker, and we are guiding his thinking, you might say," concluded Ne Xing with a measure of satisfaction.

Gene Sperling, at that moment, was reviewing statistics provided by the People's Republic of China, which clearly led to the conclusion that moving the Anniston operation to China would eventually increase shareholder value.

This will silence those old guard guys who turn their backs on international opportunities, he thought. Global competition forces us to make this move. There's my main argument, he told himself.

Two Chinese agents, along with Suzy, Gene Sperling's recent handpicked Asian resource manager, and He Fat, who had kept tabs on Sperling's movements in China, were completing their own reports. "I led him by the nose around Guangzhou, and he lapped it up," she said aloud.

The short fat man with the pockmarked face, meanwhile, was finishing his log of all contacts by Sperling during his whirlwind visit. "I agree. The man never met anyone who would make him suspicious because we had him under surveillance throughout his visit," He Fat confirmed.

They obviously could not effectively control any input he might get outside of China, but at least a solid foundation was laid. There were many other companies coming to China to escape escalating costs, regulatory controls, and other constraints so that their global competitiveness would be enhanced—or so they wanted to believe.

After returning from his trip to China, Gene was considering how to sell his plan to close the Alabama plant and move the operation to China. He said to himself, there are three levels involved. First, the board must have confidence that my numbers are reality based. Second, the corporate staff functions must get behind the idea and support it from their various viewpoints. Last, the public and customer perceptions should be positive. All of this really depended on a level of trust, he thought, but how can I cultivate that level of trust among so many stakeholders?

Gene was still considered an outsider who had not yet established a positive relationship with the other board members.

One week later, he met with the key financial people: controller, treasurer, and head of his newly created office of financial planning.

"Well, boys, it looks like our company is sitting on a strategic opportunity that could position our firm as both the most profitable in the industry and a leader in production innovation. I've called you here today to give you confidential information that I want you to analyze and compare to what would happen if we passed up the opportunity."

In front of each attendee was a packet of materials containing cost estimates of running a business in Guangzhou, which purported to include all costs from raw materials through customer delivery.

"Where did these numbers come from?" asked Mahlon Beal, the company controller.

Gene smiled and said, "I developed these costs with the help of Chinese people who know more about local costs than we do sitting here on the opposite side of the world."

This was a key point. If Gene could get them to accept his projections, their analysis would easily lead them to conclude that the move to China would yield the results Gene was promising.

"We don't know these people and what assumptions underlie their estimates. Our people should go to China and verify what you were given," Mahlon said with a forceful tone. Others were nodding in agreement.

Seeing that he could lose this battle, Gene asked, "Who could go? You guys all have full-time jobs keeping our heads above water right here."

"How about sending that new gal, Claire?" suggested Mahlon. "She's a real go-getter with the financial skills, and the fact-finding trip would be an extension of what she is doing now."

The group reluctantly agreed, thinking that she could be trusted to perform a verification function. Gene was confident that she would confirm his information.

CHAPTER 7

THE NEXT DAY Gene called Claire into his office and said, "You are off to a quick start here, and you have earned an important assignment. Do it well and you will be on a fast track around here." He then explained the verification assignment.

Gene added, "You will report directly to me and only to me on this one." Gene was confident that she would try to please him and could be counted on to tilt any ambiguities in favor of his China relocation plan.

Three days later, her flight to Hong Kong was landing, and she looked forward to meeting Suzy, the new Asian manager that Gene had recently hired. Suzy, as the native, was to help her in any way possible. Suzy at that moment was concluding a phone call with her real boss, who expected Suzy to persuade Claire to accept all of the numbers Gene had brought back from China.

Back in New York, Gene felt he had sidestepped his major concern and that, once the verification was completed, everyone would fall in line and his proposal would be approved. Approval would mean a substantial bonus for him and would also assure his continued tenure as CEO.

Einar, Claire's boss, had learned that she would be working for Gene directly, at least for this project, and he was furious. He did not trust Claire, but more importantly he was greatly concerned that the approach to evaluating this proposal was seriously flawed, but he could do nothing about it.

Claire was feeling the jet lag, having just crossed the International Date Line. Claire had now moved up, temporarily reporting to the CEO, rather than to a VP, at least on this project. She was bothered by the idea that she was not entirely free to conduct her own analysis. She felt she was being coerced into accepting facts that she could not confirm by herself. Her role was to be more that of a clerk going through a check list.

On the other hand, she thought, maybe this is reasonable. How can I be expected to go into another culture with no language skills or familiarity with business practices and come up with reliable numbers upon which to base a multimillion-dollar decision? But if I merely accept what Suzy and her Chinese cohorts tell me, I am not really verifying anything. There seemed to be no middle road, or was there?

"Yes, this is she," Claire said into her cell phone soon after checking into her hotel. The next words she heard were, "This is Einar in New York."

"Glad to hear a familiar voice," she replied, but wondered why he would be calling her considering she was no longer in his chain of command.

After an exchange of pleasantries, Einar's tone turned serious, "I am taking a risk jumping in here, and I hope you will keep this call just between us."

"Of course," she automatically replied, then wondered where this was going.

Einar explained that he had met with several unnamed others, and together they had decided to ask Claire to hire Marks & Mears, a blue-chip British consulting firm, to help her with the verification assignment. He explained that corporate accounting would pay for the services contract, but that Gene wouldn't need to know about it.

There was a long pause. Einar said, "Are you still there?"

"Yes, yes," she replied, but unable to decide what to say next.

Bringing in an outside consultant certainly made sense, she thought, but it would be a breach of trust with Gene for whom she was working directly.

Finally, she said, "I will meet with their Hong Kong office and see how we might work together on this."

Einar replied, "Excellent, and, oh, by the way, do it without the knowledge or participation of those Chinese people that Gene was running around with over there."

That call would keep Claire thinking most of the night. She thought, I could call Gene and ask if he would agree, maybe pretending it was my idea, but, no, he would not agree. Then the adage, sometimes it is better to ask forgiveness than permission, crossed her mind.

By the dawn's early light, she decided to follow up carefully with Marks & Mears and negotiate a very short service contract in the beginning. Then she called Suzy and said that she had had a terrible night, was sick, and would need two days, at least, before getting together. Suzy graciously wished her a speedy recovery.

"Marks & Mears, how may I direct your call?"

Claire gave the receptionist the name of Colin Dunlop whom Einar had provided to her.

"So nice to hear from you, Ms. Perkins. Yes, of course, we should get together, but carefully as you are probably being watched."

Watched? This struck Claire as ridiculous, but she went along with it and agreed that she would be picked up by a car two blocks from her hotel shortly after seven that evening.

Suzy, meanwhile, had taken the day off because her appointment with Claire was unexpectedly called off. No need to shadow her as she had just arrived and visitors often needed time to adjust.

The car picked up Claire, as arranged. After being dropped at a small restaurant, Claire was instructed to go directly inside where Mr. Dunlop would be waiting for her.

"Ms. Perkins, I presume," said a tall gentleman with a charming British accent. "Let's grab that booth in the back." Following a few general words about the scope of Marks & Mears activities in this part of the world, Dunlop asked quite directly, "Do you have any idea what you've gotten yourself into?"

Claire then sat openmouthed as he explained the degree of devious behavior that often accompanied the efforts of the Chinese government to induce companies to relocate operations there. Dunlop then explained that he could help her company to develop accurate and complete information that should be able to support a wise decision as to whether relocating a plant to China would make sense. His firm had done it before for other Western companies.

Claire decided to ask him how she could convince her boss that it was her work and not that of Marks & Mears, or of some other organization. At this point, she also told him about the conflicts within her company concerning the possible move to China.

A proposal was quickly agreed upon between them for Marks & Mears to independently verify the information that Gene had given to Claire and add anything that may have been overlooked. Meanwhile, Claire would proceed with her original verification assignment and report her results back to Gene, as she had been instructed to do.

Colin then concluded the meeting by telling Claire, "This meeting never took place, but we will be in contact as the need arises."

The next morning she slept late and took a walk to clear her head and think through her situation. It would now be difficult to work with the mysterious Suzy, whom Colin had described as a likely Chinese agent. She would, however, have the advantage of having been forewarned as to the manipulative style that could be expected. Diligently challenging almost everything that was explained to her and not drawing conclusions without adequate information was the only rational way of dealing with this situation, concluded Claire.

Never in her Dartmouth days had she been taught how to deal with such a complicated web of personalities, motivations, and dubious facts. Claire was beginning to realize the high-stakes game of which she was now an unwitting participant.

While she prepared to finally meet Suzy and begin her verification assignment, Colin had resumed another aspect of his job. He was reviewing intercept pages from programs that run twenty-four hours a day to capture data from thousands of organizations around the world, which were believed to have information of military or commercial value. The People's Liberation Army, from a building in Shanghai, had thousands of employees who were literally vacuuming up information that might advance China, scientifically, economically, militarily, or commercially.

At six feet, with brown hair and broad shoulders that rose above a trim waistline, Colin was aging gracefully and was highly regarded in his profession. His job had evolved from analyzing statistics to making reports back to MI6 in London as to the content of Chinese intercepts.

Now, six years later, priorities had changed. Basically, he had the responsibility to help multinationals realistically evaluate business opportunities in China. Colin relished the personal interaction that this job offered compared to his former position of analyzing statistics each day.

Three years earlier, a classified US State Department document had been approved by the president that specifically said no intelligence-gathering operations would be conducted by any of the sixteen US intelligence agencies on Chinese soil. Naval intelligence, however, would continue to monitor the buildup of China's navy. The air force would likewise continue its surveillance. Exchange of information treaties with other countries would be relied upon as the primary source of information from inside China.

This seemingly strange policy was motivated by a desire not to offend the Chinese who continued to be the biggest buyers of American government debt obligations. The United States was now highly dependent on its sale of bonds to finance its enormous debt and the government's activities.

Colin had come to his present post after responding to an ad in the *Daily Mail* that sought applicants for "governmental statistical analysis." Hardly an inviting title, but job finding was highly competitive, particularly for a University of South Hampton graduate with middling grades. Somehow he had gotten the job and soon was thoroughly immersed in number crunching. The first glow faded relatively quickly, which, in turn, led him to apply for a position in the foreign office doing essentially the same thing.

London was expensive even living in a small flat in Finsbury Park, sharing expenses with his girlfriend, Fiona. During his last months in London, Colin had gradually disengaged himself psychologically if not physically from her. She had not seen the break between them coming because she had been engrossed in her own career, working long hours as a mortgage broker for a building society.

Colin's announcement of his imminent move to Hong Kong had been met with both surprise and anger on Fiona's part because he had not kept her informed about this possibility.

Timing is often everything, and soon he had befriended a crown appointee, with impeccable peerage, who was preparing for an Asian assignment. Colin was now working for that same individual in Hong Kong. He loved the exotic atmosphere and was diligently studying Mandarin Chinese.

Back in Manhattan, Gene was hoping that his ploy of sending Claire to verify his China information would save the project to relocate in China. The other senior executives did not appear to be discussing this project, and he concluded that they all were simply waiting for Claire's verification report.

Gene focused on more routine business and his budding relationship with Sonja who might become his third wife. She would be window dressing, but he knew that she was aware of that also. An image is what he knew how to sell. Gene knew also that there was a disconnect between his perception of management and that of those executives who came up through the ranks in the company. Closing that gap had proven to be a bigger challenge than he had foreseen.

Gene's flair for publicity and hiring outsiders to perform new and questionable functions had not generated any positive movement in the company's stock price. A sense of isolation enveloped Gene as he felt a growing distance and lack of trust from the other key executives. His bold initiative to move the plant to China would show them that he had the vision to reposition the company for a dynamic rebirth.

Colin had asked for a short meeting with Claire before she returned to New York. He wanted to know how her "verification" had gone and whether she had learned anything significant that had not been in Gene's report.

"So, how did the week with Suzy go?" asked Colin.

Claire looked exhausted with deep circles under her eyes that even makeup could not hide. "I did what was asked of me," she replied. "The information that they threw at me had flaws, but not in major ways, so I can tweak Gene's report a bit, and no one will be the wiser. I can add a few things that did not occur to him."

Colin's firm had been conducting a parallel investigation of its own as to whether the relocation to China would be in the best interests of the company. "Yes, we came to roughly the same conclusion, so the issue of moving the operation here is closer to being on the line than it was before you arrived."

"I've not been in touch with Gene, but I'm sure he will be anxious to see my report," said Claire.

"How will you explain the differences between his initial report and yours?" Colin asked.

"Those differences are mostly in projections of future things, basically judgment calls. I'm just being more conservative and included some new facts. A few other items were changed when I questioned Suzy's assumptions, and she conceded that perhaps she was a bit too optimistic here and there."

"So what would you guess that your board would decide when it comes up for a vote?" Colin asked.

"I'd say it's hard to predict, but probably other factors will influence the decision."

"Well, your flight leaves in two hours, so you'd better get a move on."

Claire was leaving Hong Kong unsure of how well she could conceal her dealings with Colin. She wondered how Gene would react to her verification report and where all of this might take her career.

In China, others were reporting back to their handlers. "She questioned almost everything I said and showed to her. She was tough, but the questions were fair," said Suzy to her boss. "I have not seen her final report as she intended to finish it on the flight to New York. She did say that other factors would play a role in the company's decision, so I have no idea what will be decided."

Yet another report was being orally presented in a secure section of the Marks & Mears office in Hong Kong.

"You did your job, Colin, and now it's out of our hands. Send a short message to London, not more than two paragraphs, to sum it up and get back to your backlog," said the MI6 station chief.

CHAPTER 8

EINAR WAS TENSE as he boarded a flight from Alabama back to New York. His trip to the plant was intended to shore up morale and, at the same time, to assess the fallout to the community from a possible closure of the plant—two somewhat contradictory objectives. He had a sinking feeling that Claire would seek to please Gene for her own personal benefit. I promised to put off retirement until this deal is done, he reminded himself. Anniston would be hurt, but some of the guys who were willing to relocate could be absorbed at other locations. He resolved to fight hard for fair severance packages and that was about all he could do at this point.

Just as he got seated on the plane, his cell phone rang. It was an unfamiliar number, but the area code was 205. That's Alabama, he thought.

"Hey, Einar, it's Jimmy from the plant." Einar recognized the voice from his early days with the company.

"Great to hear your voice, Jimmy. What can I do for you?"

"Yeah, man, it was hard to get your cell number, but I got it," replied Jimmy.

"How are you?" replied Einar.

"I'm the same as ever, but the big question is how will I be next year? We were tight man, and the guys asked me to try to reach you and find out the real story on what's going down."

Einar knew he had to respond truthfully. "It doesn't look good at the moment. I can't say much more than that, but, of course, it's not a done deal yet."

"What can we do down here?" Jimmy asked.

"Let me think about that, and I'll call you in a few days, promise. Got to go now."

Jimmy was left with a disconnected phone and was disappointed with his brief chat with Einar. Was the man no longer a friend of Anniston? he wondered. Einar settled into his seat for takeoff and thought, I've got to do something, but what?

"The man shut me down," said Jimmy to his buddies in the lunchroom who were anxiously waiting for a report of his phone call to Einar.

"What did he say?"

"That it don't look good, that's what he said." The others looked on with downcast faces.

"Let's go talk to human resources," someone said.

"They don't know nothing more than we do, and even if they did, they wouldn't tell us," said someone else.

"They're treating us like a bed of mushrooms—keeping us in the dark and feeding us shit," said another.

Bob Bowers was listening to all of this moaning and groaning, but he suddenly stood up and said, "Yes, there is. We can make our case. Let's find out what this relocation looks like, as our board of directors will see it, and then present our case for staying here. We know the details of what goes on here, and we can make offers to save costs, increase productivity, and improve our safety record. I am sure they will give us a chance to at least present our case."

Bob was normally an introverted guy who focused on managing the plant's electrical grid and surprised even himself by making this bold declaration.

The guys in the lunchroom looked stunned. For a moment everybody just went silent and seemed lost in a fog. Finally, Jimmy said, "He's right, they gotta give us a chance to make our case. It's only fair." Other began to mumble in agreement.

A week later, in another "lunchroom" farther north, looking out over Central Park, a group of white-haired gentlemen in tailored suits were speaking in hushed voices.

"Well, we all read it, but what are we going to do about it?" asked Einar. "Isn't this what we are paid to do? Get the facts and then make good decisions," he continued.

"Claire put the ball squarely in our court," said Bill Harnett, the senior board member, "and we have got to put our heads together and make good long-term decisions. Her verification report identified some overstatements of cost savings and cast doubt on the rosy picture for future sales, but the bottom line is that moving to China can be expected to increase shareholder value."

"Gene must be having a fit," said another executive attendee. "Makes him lose some credibility, that's for sure. Claire must be at least halfway out the door by now."

"She's back on my team now," interjected Einar, "and I plan on keeping her around if only to explain how her report was prepared. Unfortunately, her loyalties seem to run personally to Gene," he added with a scowl.

The independent report written by Marks & Mears seemed to be closer to Claire's analysis than to Gene's initial report. However, none of these reports leaned in favor of staying in Alabama. All three, to varying degrees, supported the China relocation.

The marketing department had been asked to interview customers and determine if they had any reason to object to the products coming from China, assuming that the quality would be unchanged. The fundamental key issue was whether the labor savings would be outweighed by increased shipping and insurance costs.

"We want to pass along to you our cost savings from a possible shift of production location," Tim Jones, a regional salesperson, was explaining to one long-term customer.

"If you pass the savings to your customers, how does that benefit your firm?" the customer asked.

"We need to lower the costs to meet competition in order to keep our existing customers, and we see a large potential market in China and elsewhere in Asia also," Tim replied.

"Can you guarantee that there will be no disruption of delivery during the transition, credit terms will not change, and technical support will not be affected?" asked the customer.

"Yes, and we can even do that in writing, if you like," said Tim with a salesman's smile.

"We would certainly value such a written assurance," replied his customer.

Tim then wondered if he had gone too far by offering an assurance in writing. Yet most other customers were responding in similar ways.

Ira Horowitz, the company's general counsel, was finishing up a meeting with Gene. "This whole deal is creating a host of new legal risks that no one can begin to evaluate. China's commercial laws are barely in their infancy, and it's anyone's guess as to how any dispute over there might be resolved. Already, I am being asked by marketing to issue reassurances to our existing customers that this thing will not negatively affect them."

Gene thought, two weeks ago I would have guessed that this project would be a slam dunk, but not now. How can I get this thing back on track? he wondered.

"Ira, sometimes we have to take some risks in order to make some gains. Where would we be today if the allies had not risked the D-Day invasion to win World War II?"

Ira felt insulted by this simplistic analogy. He left the meeting intending to identify any and all legal risks that he could find that might result from a move to China.

"Did you send all three reports to Alabama?" Einar asked Margie, his admin.

"Yesterday by FedEx and to the union stewards separately," replied Margie. "These reports were marked *Company Proprietary—Not for Outside Distribution*. All of the recipients were, in fact, on the company payroll."

"We want them to be in the loop all the way to the end," Einar stated with conviction. Gene's report, Claire's report, and a summary of an independent report represented the sum total of what the board would consider. Let them see what we are dealing with up here, thought Einar, and it may provide some ideas as to how they can best make their case to stay in business.

Gene, meanwhile, was busy seeking new angles to support the move to China.

"Come in, Charlie, I'm always glad to see the guy who figures out how we can keep our taxes down," Gene said as he shook Charlie's hand.

"Nice to see you too, sir. You know we're always working to minimize the company's tax costs," said Charlie with a smile, hoping to establish a positive rapport.

"Charlie, normally we would probably meet once a year to review the tax returns before I sign them, but today I need your help on a special project."

Charlie nodded, and Gene continued, "Many big companies, like ours, try to improve their competitive position by shifting some operations overseas. We've been exploring this idea for our Alabama production facility. Maybe a move to China would give us an edge, lower labor costs, and maybe also expand our markets abroad at the same time. We also think that there may be some tax savings by moving some production overseas."

Gene then looked expectantly at Charlie.

"It's certainly worth looking at. Other companies have improved their bottom lines by going overseas, at least in the short term," said Charlie.

"Short term only?" replied Gene.

"It's tough to quantify accurately because of all the variables involved, but, generally, we would lower income tax on the profits of the overseas plant assuming the foreign corporate rates were lower than in the US, but when we bring the profits back to the states, we would end up paying taxes on the dividends from the overseas subsidiary location. And that would bring us basically back to what we are paying now. Of course, we gain a deferral on the tax until we do bring it back, and by deferring the tax, we achieve a cash-flow advantage because of the time value of money."

There was a long pause while Gene absorbed this information, then he asked, "What happens if we did not repatriate the profits back to the US?"

"Then there would be no additional US tax, but there would, probably, be foreign tax on whatever income might be generated on the investment of those offshore profits. There would also be a Social Security tax savings on the salary costs shifted overseas, but perhaps that other country has something similar."

Charlie continued, "Some companies keep the funds permanently overseas and use them to fund growth outside the US through loans and sometimes capitalizing new subsidiary companies. In fact, as you may know, this is a big political issue. Why, there are literally trillions of dollars legally kept offshore that avoid US taxation."

"Thanks for the lesson in tax policy, Charlie, but tell me this," said Gene. "Do you think that our overall tax cost would likely be less with the Alabama plant in China?"

"I don't claim to know anything about the taxation in China, but if we looked at it short term, probably there would be significant savings, but if you factor in the costs of bringing the profits back to the USA, then it might be a wash, forgetting for the moment the deferral advantage of keeping the profits outside of the US."

Gene smiled and then replied, "Would you give me a report, quantifying the savings on this relocation, but keep it within that short-term time horizon. Work with Claire Perkins to get the background. She probably can even give you the Chinese tax estimates. Can you give me a reasonably accurate report within a week?"

"I'll get something to you by then," Charlie said.

"Good, Charlie, I knew I could count on you, and please keep this project confidential, just between us." Gene then thought, if tax savings are added to the labor savings, that should more than offset all these other considerations that are being raised against the move to China.

Charlie called Claire, and they agreed to meet the next day to organize the research for the report due in one week. Claire was surprised that Gene wanted tax input because he rarely looked below the sales and operating expense lines of any financial statement. Obviously he was aggressively looking for ammunition to swing the analysis back in favor of moving to China.

OK, she thought, I'll cooperate on this. After all, it is the after-tax income that really is the true measure of profitability. She had decided to maintain a professional approach to this project and not try to sway the analysis one way or another. This might cost her a positive relationship with the CEO, but her survival seemed to dictate this more objective course of action. Who knows, she thought, maybe she could rebuild her relationship with Einar who, after all, was her boss—the person who would write her performance review.

Gene was also reflecting. Had he made a mistake by leading the charge on this move to China? By acting so decisively, he knew his reputation would take a big hit if this deal fell through. He also knew, however, he had no options now except to follow through and win the vote of the board. Sell the board and my reputation will soar; lose it and I may be out on the street, he glumly thought.

CHAPTER 9

CLAIRE WAS BACK working for Einar again and trying to rebuild her relationship with him. Now he was sending her back to Alabama to receive all of the "ammunition" that was being assembled in support of keeping the plant open.

"You wanted to see me, boss?" asked Claire. The word *boss* was spoken with a smile, which Einar took to be an effort to restore a positive relationship.

"Yes, I did, but wish you had come by earlier because I wanted you to meet someone who will be going to Anniston at the same time as you. He's gone now, but you should arrange to at least meet him before you leave—next Tuesday, is it?"

"Yes, New York to Washington, then a commuter flight to Birmingham."

"Yes, yes, I know that route well. Well, his name is George Tazikis, and he works for our outside auditors and has been assigned to conduct a plant audit, which is normal procedure when the company is contemplating something like this. Claire, I do want you to help him get around down there. He has never been there. Also, if he asks you anything relating to his audit, you need to give him straight answers. It's in our auditors' contract. You each have separate missions, but there is some overlap."

Claire brightened at the thought of not being the only Yankee down there. She reached George by cell phone, and they agreed to meet the day after tomorrow in Claire's office.

Three days after their meeting, George and Claire were flying to Alabama. Their plane was delayed by two hours due to bad weather on the West Coast, although their flight path had no such prediction of bad weather. Go figure, thought Claire, as she and George wearily exited the commuter connection from Washington to Birmingham.

Gene had told her, "Claire, people down at that plant are stirring up trouble. They're desperate to make a case for keeping the plant in Anniston. Your earlier trip and other research have revealed the true state of things. Go down there, listen to them, all of them. Don't argue with them. Then let me know what are the weak points of their case against the relocation."

What about the strong points? Claire wondered, but she kept silent.

"Ms. Perkins, it's so nice to see you again, and this must be Mr. Tazikis," said a smiling Jimmy, who had driven her during her first trip. He quickly took their bags to the van, and soon they were driving along US 20 toward Anniston.

"How long you going to be with us this time, Ms. Perkins?" asked Jimmy.

"As long as it takes," she replied, rather matter-of-factly. Claire judged it unwise to be drawn into any conversations as to what the thinking might be in New York, her own views, or anything upon which she might be quoted. A little friendly chitchat with Jimmy should be safe enough. George remained quiet, soaking in the unfamiliar northern Alabama barren rural landscape.

"Because your flight was way late, I'm going to need to stop by my place before I drop you at the hotel," Jimmy said.

Claire soon nodded off. Forty minutes later, they slowed to a halt, and Claire woke up to see that they were now in a moderate-income black neighborhood. Small single story brick homes built on slabs lined the street. The only variation seemed to be whether or not the front yards were well maintained.

Jimmy said, "Come on in and meet my family 'cause it might take a few minutes." They climbed out of the van thinking it was better to stick with Jimmy than to sit alone outside.

"Momma, this is the lady I was telling you about, all the way from New York City, and this is her friend George."

The two ladies smiled at each other. One young, tall, and elegantly dressed and the other much older, full-bodied, and dressed in red sweat pants with a 'Bama T-shirt and flip-flops.

"You must be hungry after all of that traveling," Jimmy's mother said. "Take a chair at the table and join us for some real Southern cooking."

Claire smiled again and thought, why not. A small bag of peanuts and a small Diet Coke was all she had had in the last five hours.

The ham with collards, corn bread, and black-eyed peas were served up with sweet ice tea, and soon the conversation turned to questions about life in the Big Apple. Carolyn, Jimmy's mother, was full of questions about the big city. No, Claire did not know Donald Trump. The Statute of Liberty was indeed a sight to behold, and, yes, the cost of living was sky high.

Claire was charmed by the casual atmosphere and the unrestrained flow of questions, which she could easily answer. No tension or pressure here, she thought. If only the rest of this trip would be the same. An hour later, they reached the hotel check-in counter at the quaint Victoria Inn on Quintard Avenue.

"Three messages for you, Ms. Perkins," said the smiling desk clerk, as he handed them to her.

Claire scanned the slips. One from the chief union steward who was confirming a breakfast meeting the next morning, which would include several plant representatives. A second from the plant HR manager, and the last from the director of the local Chamber of Commerce. There were no messages for George.

Lord, just let me get through this, she said to herself, recognizing that they were going to try to squeeze any and all information out of her. She was here to get information from them and not vice versa.

Things generally start early in Alabama, maybe by tradition, and maybe because the days heat up quickly. Three middle-aged white men in coats and ties were chatting amicably around a big coffee pot when Claire entered the hotel's buffet breakfast room. Clean plates were neatly piled before the array of steam table offerings.

"Well, well, this pretty young lady must be Claire," said the older of the three, as he extended a smile and a handshake. "That's me," she replied with a forced smile.

All three looked like they might be related. Each had a pot belly which hung slightly beyond the belt line. Their age differences seemed to be defined by their heights and their hairlines. The tallest one, with the most hair, was obviously the youngest and the balding short one was clearly the oldest.

"It is indeed a pleasure to welcome you to our fair city and hope that you find it to your liking," declared the oldest one.. After her first visit, six months earlier, Claire was expecting this type of verbose courtesy and did not take it as patronizing. Names were exchanged and it seemed clear that the oldest, Roy, would do most of the talking. The four filled their plates at the buffet and chose a table in the rear of the room away from the clatter of dishes.

"The big boys up in New York really got this place on edge, Ms. Perkins," continued Roy. He explained that he had represented the plant employees for over twenty years and now the union headquarters in Washington was following every detail of the turmoil in Anniston.

The others nodded in agreement and looked expectantly at Claire.

"First, understand that I'm not a decision-maker, I'm only here to collect information," she said. "The boys in New York, as you call them, want to hear from you. That's why I'm here, to get your message and deliver it to them."

"We've collected some information that's relevant and believe has been overlooked," Roy explained.

"Good, that's what I'm here for," Claire repeated, with a measured smile.

At that same moment, George was just waking up and would go directly to the plant controller's office after a quick breakfast from room service. He and Claire had agreed to meet and compare notes that evening because their paths were not expected to cross during the day.

Claire and George decided to have dinner at 7:00 p.m. in the hotel dining room, which had a pleasant, subdued atmosphere with pictures of sights from around the state.

"Catfish, hush puppies, and the salad bar make a wonderful supper," said a teenaged waitress with a friendly grin. They both agreed to that. Soon the conversation turned to what each of them had done that day.

"I had an audit plan faxed down here, but they couldn't find it, so I had to explain the details to them," said George. "Beyond discussing what was to be done, we did not really make much progress. I did meet the cost accountant, cash manager, and the controller. They all seemed like nice fellows. Willing to help."

Then Claire began, "Well, my day was exhausting. I was on the defensive from the get-go. First, it was a history lesson on the community and the plant's long involvement here. Then a statistics course about the impact if the plant closed. I don't know how accurate all of that really was, but the conclusions were dire."

She had evaded all leading questions, but tomorrow would be tougher as the union representatives would press her. They had a right to at least some answers under the collective bargaining agreement.

Tomorrow George expected to verify existing inventories while the remaining audit items were being assembled for his review. They returned to their rooms to get some sleep before the next day.

Claire, however, was mulling over the exchange of personal information that she had had with George who, she learned, was a CPA with an MBA from NYU. She felt somewhat superior with her Ivy League credentials, but he had impressed her with his good manners, big smile, and sparkling personality. They were the same age, but he was much more practically grounded with two years in the army and working as a waiter in a Greek restaurant, which his uncle apparently owned.

She, on the other hand, had a purely academic background with not even a summer job along the way. After her adventure with Gene Sperling, George, by comparison, seemed equally self-assured, but with a sincerity that Gene lacked. Wonder what his social life is like, she pondered as she dozed off for the night.

The union hall was two blocks from the plant and seemed rather shabby compared to the company's New York headquarters. The floors were bare linoleum; faded, dusty curtains kept the sun out; and there were tobacco stains on the ceiling over the conference table. Almost immediately she was introduced to more people than she could possibly remember.

"We have prepared a report for you, Ms. Perkins, which explains some things about your employees, their safety record, their loyalty, and their honesty about which you may be unaware." The spokesperson was a lawyer for the union and was obviously gearing up for a formal presentation replete with PowerPoint visuals.

Comparisons with other plants in the same industry showed a relatively lower accident rate, almost no pilferage, low employee turnover, and fewer grievance filings than comparable plants.

"The bottom line, Ms. Perkins, is that there is an atmosphere of trust here, which has translated into an efficient operation over an extended period of time that we doubt can be duplicated in China or anywhere else," the union lawyer concluded.

All eyes now shifted to Claire.

"I will be happy to bring all of these materials back to corporate headquarters.

They will be considered, I assure you," she said.

"Why can't any of these big-shot decision-makers come down here and talk to us face to face?" asked a younger employee who had remained silent up until now.

"It's too preliminary, and Einar, who spent many years of his career here, will come here before any final decision is made. He asked me specifically to tell you this."

While Claire was being grilled by the union representatives at their office, George was standing next to a large commercial storage vat at the plant that contained chemicals ready to be pumped into smaller containers, which would be sold to customers. The fumes were overpowering despite his wearing a respirator. This was "work in progress," according to accounting definitions, and George felt confident that the product was all there.

Reviewing accounts receivable and payables would be a piece of cake after dripping in sweat while measuring thousands of gallons of chemicals. He looked forward to a shower and meeting Claire for dinner at the usual time. George hoped that they would find time to explore more personal interests. After all, what interest would she have in how chemical inventories were counted?

That night Claire and George met in the hotel lobby to decide where to go for a casual dinner.

"Today there was more pressure," began Claire. "I had to tell the union people what I knew about the possibility of moving the plant overseas. Fortunately, I didn't know much, only that it was being explored. So, how was your day, George?"

"Well, all of the chemicals listed as inventory appear to be there. Let's talk about something else." Then he added, "Do you like Greek food?"

"Love it," she responded with enthusiasm.

"Great, we're going to Gus's Greek Restaurant, which is about ten minutes from here. Their moussaka is highly recommended by the natives," replied George.

Sensing that Claire was feeling stressed, George decided to lighten the mood with a few tales of his online dating adventures.

"Usually, we meet at coffee shops to get acquainted," he explained. "One time, a girl insisted that I meet her at a funeral home. It turned out that she was on call there where she worked as a cosmetologist for the cadavers. Another time, about ten minutes after meeting, the girl asked me if I had been saved. Saved from what I replied? She then gave me some literature and tried to convert me to her religion."

Claire was soon laughing at George's dating adventures, but then began to wonder if maybe she should give it a try. She asked how he was enjoying being an auditor for a big accounting firm. Finally, she asked him about his family life and hobbies.

George had little time for outside activities at the present time, but hoped that when things lightened up he could get back into tennis and racquetball. At this moment his recreation was limited to occasional movies, which he always enjoyed. George had grown up on Staten Island. His father was a policeman and his mother a seamstress. He had one brother who had been killed on 9/11 while working for a brokerage firm in the World Trade Center.

They both conceded that, at the moment, their social lives were almost nonexistent despite George's computer-dating. Claire gave him a sincere smile that she hoped communicated that she was open to exploring whether they could be more than business associates. They both agreed that sacrifices now would make for a better future in the longer term.

Since this was George's first trip to Alabama and to the South, in general, Claire thought that she would share what she had learned about the Anniston area. George was a bit of a history buff and warmed to the topic.

Basically, Anniston has been on a downhill roll ever since the Union Army destroyed its iron foundry during the Civil War. Pipe, either in the form of iron, steel, or clay, often called "soil pipe," continued to be the industrial base of the local economy for many years, however.

Anniston was frequently in the news during the 1960s, first in 1961, when a bus carrying Freedom Riders was blown up, and again in 1963, when violence erupted over efforts to integrate a whites-only public library. This all led to a Pulitzer Prize for Taylor Branch, who wrote about the period in a book called *At Canaan's Edge*.

Claire had obviously done her homework and continued to describe the community. "The city population has been in a slow, steady decline since the mid-1960s and now hovers at around twenty-three thousand people with nearly a balance between whites and blacks. Wages have been stagnant with a growing number of families falling below the poverty line. On my earlier trip down here, Jimmy gave me a tour that would have embarassed the local Chamber of Commerce.. That got me to do a little research which showed why these people are so desperate to keep the plant in operation."

The city's main employer today is the Anniston Army Depot, which has had quite a history of its own. It had been used for storing deadly chemical weapons, but their destruction was finally completed in 2002. Now the depot concentrates on storing and repairing military track vehicles. Nearby Fort McClellan had operated as a training facility for military police, but has now been converted to a wildlife refuge.

"Very Interesting," exclaimed George, after Claire finished her synopsis of the local scene.

"Yes, it's quite different from where you and I were brought up," she said. "Now it's easy to understand why our plant employees are so concerned about the possibility of their jobs moving to China. There are very few job opportunities here. Places like this are all over this country, and they are being bypassed because of labor costs and other considerations that make them unattractive in the global business world."

"This so-called globalization of business has generated increased competition in the quest for greater profits and economic power, which is shrinking the middle class and enriching those at the top. These people here in Alabama are feeling that impact in their daily lives," said Claire with obvious strong feelings.

George mentioned that conducting audits had given him an appreciation of this globalization trend, particularly the impact of America's taxation, legal, and accounting practices on how business is conducted and reported.

"Our American laws, accounting practices, and even ethics are being exported to other countries," he said. "Many countries outside the USA had no laws that could effectively regulate these multinational companies, so they adopted our laws, which had already been refined over many years."

"You've obviously thought through this dilemma," Claire observed.

"Yes, American tax laws, for example, have evolved in order to deal with evasive business practices, which were intended to keep tax costs to a legal minimum," George said. "Now we have tax treaties between the US and many other countries, which provide for information exchanges and also help businesses avoid double tax costs when two countries claim the power to tax the same income."

"I think that's part of our issue here," Claire said.

"It certainly has implications for this possible China move," George said. "Maybe the biggest thing in this whole area is the way our country asserts its legal power to bring activities outside of America within the power of the US legal system. Many foreign governments dispute this power, but it does force businesses to follow some legal standards.

Claire listened carefully and was impressed with George's grasp of the bigger picture.

George went on, "Ethics-wise, a foreign company owned or controlled by Americans cannot pay bribes to get business without risk of fines or jail time for the US owners. This has cost US-controlled companies a lot of sales, but gradually other countries are beginning to adopt the same rules because they serve to curb corruption."

Soon the meal and the enlightening discussion were over, and they agreed that a short nightcap was in order because there was nothing else to do before the next business day began.

Day three in Anniston began for both of them in the plant's main office. Claire was speaking to the HR people about severance provisions in the union contracts, and George was reviewing overdue accounts to determine whether the bad debt reserve was adequate. She had planned on one more day to speak with the Chamber of Commerce and then a wrap-up meeting with Billy, the plant manager. Claire knew that to stay longer might create more tension than already existed.

Jimmy had suggested Top O' the River for their last supper together. It was widely regarded as the iconic Anniston dining destination. Since they were both on expense accounts, they agreed to give it a try. At this point there was a nervous romantic expectation in both of them.

"I'd like to see you again in New York and not about business," ventured George during their dinner.

Claire reached across the table and squeezed his hand and said, "That's a great idea."

"I know you're booked tomorrow on the afternoon connection back to New York, but could we possibly meet next week in Manhattan?"

"Please call me and we'll make a date," Claire responded with a soft smile.

From the Birmingham Airport, Claire made a quick call to Einar to tell him the mood in the plant and whom she had met with.

"Sounds like you've touched all of the key bases. Let's meet in my office as soon as possible. Together, we can pull together a report summarizing the situation down there," said Einar.

That report, she knew, would be the main counterargument to the overseas relocation, but how persuasive would it really be? she wondered. Claire then thought, I started out only seeing my work in terms of how I could use it to advance my career, and now I have evolved to a point where I actually care that the end result is the best possible. In school most grades are determined by individual results on an examination. And this reward seldom takes into account teamwork. Now I'm learning to appreciate teamwork and it feels good.

CHAPTER 10

ON THE OTHER side of the world, where it was already the next day, a staff meeting was called to review the status of inquiries from foreign companies considering moving factory assets to China.

"So what is the thinking of Gene Sperling and his cohorts?" asked the senior government official..

"Two of their people visited us, including Mr. Sperling, and that was several months ago now. Do they need any further information from us? Should one of our commercial attachés in Manhattan pay a courtesy call on them?" asked the senior official.

"No, I don't think so," replied Suzy, who had met with both Gene and Claire. "We think there is some sort of a power struggle going on within the company over this issue, and it might be best not to get in the middle."

The meeting passed on to other businesses that were making similar investigations.

China had established clear goals: to generate new jobs for the people moving into the cities, to update technology, and to secure more foreign investment. Factory relocations from abroad served all of these purposes and were a high government priority.

Back from her second trip to Alabama, Claire was seated at her office computer.

"Time passes quickly when you're having fun," said Gene as he leaned into Claire's doorway. She looked up from her computer where she was preparing her second Anniston trip report. It was quite unusual for the CEO to be paying unannounced visits to the offices of staff employees.

He slid into the one straight-backed chair in Claire's office and asked with a smile, "So, how did it go?"

"Three days was enough to get their facts and arguments," she replied. Anticipating what he was after, she added, "But I didn't find any smoking guns or bodies in the cellar."

"Just what did you find?" Gene asked in a surprisingly stern tone.

Claire reviewed with him her notes of meetings with the union people, HR, Chamber of Commerce, and the plant manager and then added that George's audit apparently confirmed that the accounting was in proper order.

"What do you think they were hiding?" asked Gene with a bit of a sneer.

"We could challenge a few underlying assumptions, but basically the plant seems to be operating efficiently and—" Gene stood up, cutting her off in midsentence, and abruptly left her office without a further word.

He is really upset that I didn't find something that would give him ammunition to support the relocation, she thought. His sudden change in attitude scared her because she had not seen it before.

Although her report and the audit by George showed Anniston in a favorable light, the cost savings in China would still sway the analysis decidedly in favor of relocation.

Gene's angry at me, but Einar is now my buddy. What a flip-flop, she thought, but why can't Gene simply stop pushing this relocation and take a more neutral stance? What's motivating him?

Gene settled into his leather and chrome office chair and thought, I gave that bitch preferential treatment, and she still didn't back me up. Surely something's not going well down there, but she avoided reporting it. Whose team is she on? he wondered.

His mask of goodwill was beginning to fracture, and he could sense it. Without that image to project, Gene knew that his days would be numbered. Only he and the two members of the board who were on the compensation committee knew that a $3-million bonus would be his if he relocated the plant operations overseas.

At that time the board had been caught up in the frenzy to position assets where they could yield the best return or risk losing their market position due to cost disadvantages. The bonus was set up to strongly motivate the new CEO to aggressively pursue that option—thinking, at the time, that it would be crucial to the company's survival.

Gene had taken the bait, and now he felt that he had no choice but to force the move. Another incentive had been secretly conveyed under the table by the Chinese Industrial Development Board.

"If you can orchestrate the plant move to China, we will put five million US dollars into a Swiss bank account for you when the move is completed," Gene was promised. Eight-million dollars can buy a lot of motivation, and now Gene had gone all out, but the momentum seemed to be going against him. The emerging facts were now his enemy, and he felt he had to beat them down by any means necessary. Gene picked up the phone and dialed a number he had been given. "Yes, tonight, if possible," he said and then wrote down the address.

He would renegotiate. The $5 million hopefully could be exchanged for $3 million, if he at least delivered a strong board recommendation, which he would tell the Chinese would be almost as good and for $2 million less. Once that change was made, he would demand the $3-million bonus from the board because of his hard work to make the relocation a reality. If they balked, he would threaten a lawsuit for breach of contract. This way, win or lose, he hoped to get $6 million and then retire. Any risk of jail time seemed so unlikely that it never entered his thinking.

CHAPTER 11

Two time zones to the west, a seemingly unrelated military project was under way. Kirtland Air Force Base outside Albuquerque, New Mexico, is the headquarters for the air force's nuclear weapons. Two pilots stationed there were settling into chairs in a small conference room to be briefed on an upcoming mission.

Captain Bob Reilly no longer enjoyed the thrills of air combat maneuvers and was looking forward to moving over to commercial aviation. The other pilot, Josh Wackerman, had recently been assigned to take pictures of test missions performed by other pilots.

Colonel Manning, with coffee cup in hand, was a tall, robust man who could no longer pass the medical exam required of military pilots. The three shook hands, and then Manning proceeded with his briefing.

"Tomorrow, Bob, you will test fire a new kind of missile. It will be done not here in New Mexico but in a remote part of Nevada, east of China Lake. The design for the warhead curiously enough, came from the army. They called it Davy Crockett," Manning said.

The two pilots leaned in to hear more.

"It's the smallest nuclear warhead in our arsenal. During the height of the Cold War, it was issued to infantry troops in Germany who were preparing to stop any possible Soviet attack in Western Europe. Problem was that it was inaccurate, and there was always the possibility that the wind could change and blow nuclear fallout back into our troops. This program is being run from here at the Nuclear Weapons Center because of the nature of the ordnance being delivered. That's about it. Any questions?" Manning wrapped up the briefing.

After the briefing, both pilots were struck by the broader implications of a nuclear device of such small size. The risks of proliferation seemed much greater with something like this. It could easily be concealed in a suitcase and transported by an individual just about anywhere.

Neither the pilots, nor Colonel Manning, knew or would be interested to know that the warheads were assembled in a small building at a chemical plant in Alabama.

CHAPTER 12

BACK IN NEW YORK City, near Washington Square in Greenwich Village, Claire entered a small but attractively decorated restaurant. It was the same restaurant in which George had worked and his uncle owned. Grilled lamb with garlic and mint filled her nostrils with an exotic smell that awoke her dormant appetite.

"So you made it," said George greeting her at the door. "Sit down and let's try some wine while you look at the menu. That's it in chalk on the blackboard," he said. They agreed to talk about anything but business.

"Convenient location don't you think?" he asked. Then added, with a laugh, "It took me about three minutes to get down here. I live three floors above where we are sitting."

Claire mentioned that she lived walking distance from her office and about a twenty-minute express subway ride from Greenwich Village. Soon they were discussing current theater productions. It was a small transition from there to deciding that a night at Lincoln Center together should soon be a first-time experience for both of them. George would see about obtaining tickets.

The lights had dimmed, and George walked Claire, hand in hand, in the light summer evening breeze to the top of the subway entrance. George stepped forward and wrapped his muscular arms around Claire's slender waist, and they melted together in their first kiss. Then Claire quickly went down the steps to her train without a further word or glance back at him.

Meanwhile, Gene was nervous about the appointment that he had made to talk secretly with the Chinese government official.

As he entered the restaurant on Canal Street, he was promptly escorted to a private booth where a Mr. Yu awaited him. Gene explained that he had called the meeting because he was now willing to take $3 million in exchange for his total effort to get the plant relocated in China. That would save the Chinese $2 million.

Mr. Yu replied, "We know that there is considerable conflict within your company about making this relocation, and we are interested only in results. That is why we offered the five million dollars, once the plant is moved to China. "Gene responded, "I understand that much, but the numbers still support the move, and I am confident that that is what the board will focus on. Their job, after all, is to support actions that will increase shareholder value."

"I will send your offer back to Beijing, but I don't think they'll go for it," Mr. Yu replied.

As Gene left the restaurant, his mind was spinning with self-serving thoughts. If I can eliminate, or at least neutralize, the opposition, the project will get approved, he thought. He suspected that the Chinese were unlikely to take his offer of less money for something that was not a sure thing. If Claire's Anniston report could be discredited, that should be enough to swing the necessary votes to his side.

Slowly a plan began to form in Gene's mind. He could hire a few "consultants" to visit Alabama on the pretext of reviewing quality controls and potential legal exposures. If they concluded that the plant was a disaster waiting to happen, that would create enough concern to swing the votes his way. He also could have former disgruntled employees interviewed who might be willing, possibly for a fee, to make statements about safety concerns, environmental cover-ups, or maybe discriminatory hiring practices.

There also was the possibility of planting stories in the local media about corruption at the plant. This all could be done under the label of "due diligence." Gene's mind was now focused on how this could be done. Time was short, but there was enough time to complete this smear campaign, but not enough to allow for a further investigation by his opposition. Gene's last thought before falling asleep was, who could I get to do this job?

The next morning Gene's outlook had improved after a random thought had grabbed him while shaving. Of course, he said to himself, those political hangers-on who do the background work on political candidates also do other jobs. They can find the juicy stuff on anyone, he mused. This was off-season for political campaigning, and those guys needed work, he realized.

A certain Washington, D.C, public relations firm was often called the "power house" because it had received media recognition for winning tough political campaigns for its clients. Was this project fundamentally any different? wondered Gene. He often traveled to DC on company business, so he decided to meet with that certain public relations firm that had such a powerful reputation among its clients.

"Yes," said David Kranz, the senior partner, "we have experts on retainer who can expose areas of legal risk, safety violations, and other areas that a management team might be covering up, and we can discreetly leak that information to media outlets for maximum impact at the proper moment."

Gene now felt assured he had found the right partners.

"Payment can be arranged through our Swiss affiliate," Kranz said. "We can accept short-term notes from your company because yours is a publicly traded company, and they will be easy to sell. We will then sell the notes on the open market and collect our fee. That way no cash trail will be evident."

After Gene spelled out the particular work to be performed, Kranz said, "Two million, and the job will be very professionally done."

Gene knew that he could authorize a limited amount of short-term notes for special purposes without board approval.

"Great, let's get started," Gene said in an upbeat voice.

Perched in her office chair, staring at a blank computer screen, Claire was feeling a twinge of ethics as she contemplated how things had changed. I was clearly allied with Gene when this whole thing got started and all for selfish reasons, she said to herself. Now, it's as if the angels have led me to a path that is the best solution for the company and allows me to live with myself.

Claire reflected on her college course on business ethics that she had taken only a year ago. She recalled the professor talking about a fundamental struggle between individual greed and a collective good.

CHAPTER 13

ON THE OTHER side of the world, knowledge about the recent firing of a nuclear-tipped missile in a remote part of Nevada had drawn high-level attention.

The Ministry of State Security (MSS), the key component of an intelligence apparatus, was primarily responsible for gathering both military and commercial information for China. The division was highly regarded by its peers in other countries, but generally worked in a somewhat different way than other national intelligence organizations. The MSS relied heavily upon large numbers of "amateurs" in carrying out its objectives. A second difference was that the division targeted logistical systems, which most other nations ignore in setting their intelligence priorities.

At any given time, there are roughly eighty to ninety thousand Chinese nationals in the United States. About half are students or interns. Another large group are visitors, tourists, and conference attendees. Some twenty thousand or so are immigrants, and nearly three thousand are diplomatic and commercial government employees.

Nearly all of these people have at least a secondary role in collecting information that may have strategic value to China. The largest group of foreign exchange students in the United States is Chinese. In addition, a large computer-hacking operation is run from Shanghai. in a building that is well know to other intelligence services. It is believed that these intelligence-gathering activities have been very successful over many years.

MSS monitoring in geographic areas used by the US military for testing new weapons disclosed that nuclear waste was released from an air force missile test firing in a remote part of Nevada.

Adding in routine cargo manifest information hacked from a Department of Defense database, the MSS learned that flights from Maxwell Air Force Base in Alabama to Kirtland AFB carried cargo listed as "AIM/26A/ Davy Crockett warheads." Putting the puzzle together, it soon became clear that such warheads had been assembled at a commercial chemical plant in Alabama for the army under the same name for over six years, but then production had temporarily stopped.

It seemed reasonable that the air force had now taken over the program for its own use. China immediately put this technology on its highest priority "shopping list."

He Ming of the Second Department of the PLA General Staff Headquarters had all of this information in front of him. It was his job to devise a plan to secure this technology as soon as possible. However, in this case, he discovered that China had few qualified people in that geographic area to carry out the assignment.

Intercepting the warheads as they were shipped to Kirtland for assembly into missiles would be difficult, as the air force picked up the warheads at the plant by an armored type of military vehicle and then delivered them to Maxwell AFB where they were flown directly to Kirtland. Security at Kirtland was tighter than at most air force bases because of its mission of managing and coordinating the deployment of nuclear weapons.

An MSS meeting to focus on sources and methods of obtaining the warheads was called by He Ming to decide how best to proceed.

A general from the PLA spoke first. "Speaking for the army, we have a policy of not confronting the US military in any operation that could lead directly to violence. In this case, we believe that obtaining the technology or, better yet, the warhead itself should be done at the Anniston commercial production site."

No one disagreed with the general, so the project now focused on gaining access to the assembly facility. A review of qualified Chinese presently located in the vicinity led to one Yao Son, a graduate chemistry student at the University of Alabama. His father had served in the PLA, and the son was categorized as "highly reliable."

Shortly thereafter, in New York, Mr. Yu was dialing his phone to contact Gene Sperling. Yu had recently met with Sperling to receive his offer to accept less money in exchange for his best efforts to move the plant to China, instead of a larger sum when the plant was relocated there.

"Mr. Sperling, sir, I am still awaiting for a reply from your offer, but in the meantime, I do have a small request that is somewhat of a personal favor."

"Mr. Yu, it's nice to hear your voice, and if I can be helpful to you in some way, it would be my pleasure," Gene said.

"My nephew, Yao Son, happens to be studying chemistry in Alabama and would like to get some direct exposure to the chemical industry, perhaps through an internship or some kind of work/study experience. Since you are the CEO of a chemical company with a plant in Alabama, I thought that maybe you could help in this regard."

Gene sensing that helping with a personal favor, which would cost him nothing, might help lead to the acceptance of his offer made through Mr. Yu, replied, "We're often looking for good technical people to help in our plants. Let me see what I can do. I'll get back to you."

Gene's next thought was to call Einar in and ask him about the status of internships and other forms of cooperative agreements with universities, where the company had plant locations.

Later that same day, Bill Vaalens, the Anniston plant manager, took a phone call from his boss in New York.

"OK, Einar, we might be able to take him on, but I need to figure out where he might fit in, at what pay level, and for how long. Have him give me a call, and we'll invite him in and look him over."

One week later, two officials from the MSS, operating under cover as commercial attachés approached Yao as he departed from the chemistry lab. Would he like to have coffee with two gentlemen who brought greetings from his father?

"Of course, I am honored that you contacted me," replied the normally meek Yao.

It was quickly agreed that Yao would explore the possibility of visiting the Anniston plant as part of a research project, to apply for an internship or anything else that might get him at least past the plant gate.

Two weeks later Yao Son was soon cleaning vats, filters, and mixing equipment for fifteen hours each week. It was a dirty job. He soon learned the security procedures and the location of the air force project. Reading through the plant maintenance manual, he noted that all maintenance done in Building #220, which housed the air force project, must be done either by air force personnel or plant employees. No outside contractors were allowed for security reasons.

When an opportunity for doing outdoor maintenance came up, Yao volunteered, saying that he really could use some extra money. This allowed him to roam the entire two hundred acres of the plant grounds, but it still didn't get him inside Building #220. He was, however, able to view some of the interior of that small one-story building when the cargo doors were open, which seemed to occur whenever the temperature rose into the mid-nineties. He took pictures with a special camera designed for such jobs. There was enough detail to see cylindrical tubes, roughly eighteen inches long, painted white and yellow, which were presumably the assembled warheads.

All of this information gleaned by Yao was quickly passed back to his handlers. Two weeks later, he was called to a meeting.

"Yao, you have done well to gain so much information in so short a period of time," said the older of the two men.

The younger one continued, "We have a plan that you, and only you, will carry out. It will bring honor to your family."

The gist of the plan was that Yao would be given some dormant nests of fire ants, and he would place them near all lines of electric wires, pipes, compressors, and any other connections going into Building #220. With summer heat to bring the ants to a more active level, it should take only a few weeks for the ants to penetrate the building. Yao would, by then, be knowledgeable about how to eradicate fire ants. It was considered unlikely that the air force, with its closest base being almost two hours away, would send in someone to deal with such a routine extermination problem. Yao would also begin casually mentioning to his boss that his research at the university included chemicals used to control insects, ants, and other such pests, so that he would be chosen to do the eradication when the time came. Yao knew that he had no choice. The security of his family back in China depended upon his carrying through with this risky plan.

Meanwhile, his handlers had requested technical help. A zippered blue canvas bag with straps to mount the bag on the chest of a person was fabricated. A yellow-and-white container approximately eighteen inches long, which generally matched the appearance of those cylinders photographed at Building #220, would be put inside the bag. That cylinder would contain an appropriate chemical to eradicate the fire ants. In addition, it would also contain an inert gas, which, when sprayed, would obscure for less than one minute the area being treated.

The final steps would require Yao to move close to one of the cylinders, open the zipper, and substitute his ant spray container for a warhead. He would then exit the building, walk to his car, and drive home with the device. He would try to perform the spraying late in the afternoon so that his departure would coincide with the regular shift change. Hopefully, the substituted cylinder would go unnoticed until the next morning.

The call came four weeks later. "We got a big problem with these damn ants. They're crawling all over the place. Never saw anything like it."

It took most of the day before Yao was told to exterminate the ants. He arrived twenty minutes before quitting time when most of the six employees were standing outside. He was escorted inside and began spraying immediately. Soon he was operating without supervision. He moved methodically around the one-story structure, spraying as he went. Finally he approached the area with the assembled warheads.

Yao quickly made the switch and exited the building, telling the employees, "Let that treatment settle until the morning, and then the ants should be dead." They gave him a big thumbs-up. Yao walked, with heart pounding, to his car and joined the line to pass through the plant gate with the other workers who had just finished their shifts.

By the time the dummy cylinder was discovered the next morning, Yao and his "package" were flying west across the Pacific Ocean.

CHAPTER 14

MORE INFORMATION WAS piling up that seemed to support the efficient operation of the Anniston plant, but would it be enough to keep the plant operating?

"George, I saw your audit report, and it looked pretty clean," said Einar.

"Yeah, they seem to have things under control down there, but I did make a recommendation for monitoring plant costs," replied George. "The reason I stopped by today was to ask you if, being a member of the finance committee, you know why the consolidated balance sheet today shows an increase in short-term debt of two million dollars, which was not there two days ago?"

Einar looked disturbed by this information. He should have known about such a discrepancy before it occurred. "It's a surprise to me too." he replied.

"I asked the corporate treasurer, and he's drawing a blank too," said George.

Down in Alabama, two men appearing to be ordinary business travelers were checking into a motel a short distance from Anniston. Each registered for six days. Both were consultants from the "power house" Washington, DC, public relations firm.

They had already identified potential sources of information before arriving. The list included former employees who had filed grievances with the company, local environmental activists, and all of those who had ever filed lawsuits against the company.

Gene had provided these leads by saying that he wanted to conduct an outside review of Claire's Anniston report before presenting anything to the board.

Both of these men were experienced at their craft. Each had been a strategist in political campaigns and relished finding "ammunition" that could swing voters. Here the voters would be corporate board members who had different personal biases and life experiences just like everyone else, which influenced their attitudes about making decisions.

Back in New York, two travelers stood in line to check in for their flight to Bermuda. Claire was excited and feeling a release of tensions from her work pressures. George had wangled the extended weekend after finishing his report on the mysterious $2 million of short-term notes that nobody seemed to know about. Apparently Gene had made a $2 million political campaign contribution, but had forgotten to inform the company's political action committee.

Much as an alignment of the planets was believed to predict major natural events, the work of two business visitors in Alabama, combined with the discovery of $2 million in new debt and Claire's Anniston report, were all lining up to create a seismic event that might alter the lives of many people.

A week later Gene was reading in the *Wall Street Journal* that the Anniston plant was under investigation for violating EPA rules for dumping of toxic chemicals and might face heavy fines. The same article went on to mention that apparently several minority employees had lost their jobs due to a racially motivated employee cutback, and, lastly, safety records had been fudged to present a false picture of a safer workplace. Gene's "no comment" to this article only added fuel to the growing fire.

Yes, thought Gene, the board will want to close this chapter of corporate history rather than face lawsuits, adverse publicity, and shareholder questions. A move to China will allow them to sidestep all of these messy issues.

On another front, government policy toward China was, at that moment, under review. In the large ornate building adjoining the west wing of the White House, usually called the Executive Office Building, on Pennsylvania Avenue, Dan Kiley, a member of the National Security Council staff was preparing an "eyes only" report for the president.

Dan's career had been spent as an FSO, or Foreign Service Officer, working for the State Department in embassies in six countries and finally as an ambassador in Taiwan. Then a surprise transfer to this elite policy group, which he thought of as a preretirement plum had led him to work in this center of foreign policy formulation.

Dan realized that this assignment might be the most important single project in his nearly thirty-year career, and he was keenly interested in the topic. More than thirty separate reports, embassy cables, and scholarly articles were piled on his desk. He had read through all of them as they had arrived over the past few months. Now it was his job to synthesize them into a coherent, but short narrative that would convey the broader perspective of China's efforts to establish itself as a world power.

He realized, of course, that the US policy toward China had been one of accommodation and non-confrontation. Now, Dan felt, this should be the time to recommend a more aggressive approach.

Most of the reports contained details about activities that the US media, particularly Fox News, had been reporting for years. Dan recalled from his school days at Georgetown that almost all countries advancing rapidly economically could be expected to reach a stage where they would begin to project their strength economically, politically, and militarily.

One report, for example, from the American Chamber of Commerce, contained well-documented complaints of US corporations and government laboratories. It outlined how valuable technology was being stolen by several countries either by spies working in their facilities, electronic espionage, aerial surveillance, personnel exchange programs, or even through academic exchanges.

China is believed to operate the most extensive spying network. Yes, Dan thought, it really must be faster and cheaper to steal this stuff from others than to develop it yourself.

He believed that to make a plausible case for a change in policy, particularly a long-standing one involving such an important country, which also happened to be the biggest holder of US sovereign debt, would be a near impossible task. Many prominent law firms and other organizations, with high-level access, were being well paid to roam the halls of Congress, government agencies, and think tanks to increase Chinese influence.

Dan imagined that a Pearl Harbor–sized dramatic event would be needed to really create the change that was needed. The next report on the pile from the CIA marked "top secret" outlined China's systematic efforts to gain monopolies over strategic natural resources in the developing world mainly through bribery. Zambia, in Central Africa, was a case in point. Chinese investors now controlled nearly all of that country's extensive copper ore deposits.

The entire pile of reports contained the multitude of ways that the People's Republic of China was playing the power game on a global scale. However, there was nothing that could be viewed as dramatic enough in itself to justify a major policy shift, and Dan knew it.

The next morning, while riding the Metro to work, and mulling over his seemingly impossible job assignment, a simple thought occurred to Dan. Instead of trying to find justification to achieve a particular objective, why not take the reverse tack? Why don't I take what facts I do have and write up a proposed change in policy that the facts would support? He recognized that this approach would likely lead to a more realistic recommendation.

Dan also knew, however, that such an approach would be the reverse of how foreign policy was usually formulated. More typically in his line of work, a directive would come from "on high" with a request to find data to back it up. This top-down approach inevitably led field people to cherry-pick information to justify what was to be a new policy or position on some topic and thereby become a self-fulfilling prophecy.

With his Starbucks in hand, Dan was now striding into his office focused on seeing where this new approach might lead him.

Two weeks later in the Oval Office, Malcolm Stevens, the president's National Security Adviser, was saying, "You know we have to deal with the growing tensions with China. Our larger and technologically oriented companies are a constant target for them. Rather than change governmental policy toward China directly, let's change how we regulate American-based companies operating abroad."

The president was now listening intently because this was something new, which he thought might raise fewer objections.

Malcolm continued, "We could require in the future that all US companies making military or dual-use products must make them only in the US or lose their government contracts. The president thought for a moment and then asked, "Remind me what dual-use products are."

"That's the stuff that would have both military and nonmilitary applications," replied an aide.

"Our military uses just about everything that the civilian economy uses, so how do we draw the line?" asked the president to everyone in the room.

"Ah, that's where the devil is in the details," responded Malcolm. "The Defense Department," he continued, "could write contract regulations carefully keeping the things that China covets on the inside US production–only list, and everything else could be unrestricted. Tighter rules of security would be applied to the restricted stuff and stiff penalties levied on companies that fail to safeguard their research. That's it in a nutshell, Mr. President."

"Dan," called Malcolm as he passed by the office of his staff members a few minutes later, "can I have a word with you in my office? We just sold the president on your idea, and it can be implemented without congressional authorization. We just need some regulations spelling out the details. Congratulations!"

The procurement and logistics aspects of the Department of Defense seldom played a key role in the development of strategic plans. Now regulations in that area would work to protect American technology. Carmen Mancuso, a DOD civilian lawyer, was assigned the task of writing the regulations. His first thought was to make sure that all nuclear weapons systems would be produced and stockpiled in the United States. This consideration led him to obtain a classified list of all nuclear weapon production facilities.

Oak Ridge, Hanford, and Amarillo were high on the list, but smaller, lesser known locations such as Anniston, Alabama, were also included. The draft regulations were issued in record time, and the comment period was equally short because it was believed that defense contractors would otherwise try to delay the finalization of the regulations.

Thirty days later, DOD would publish the final regulations in the *Congressional Record*. Compliance would be mandatory. Defense-related technology will hopefully be better protected. Some contractors would have to make adjustments to meet the new requirements. Shifting some production back into the United States would cause problems with unions and government officials in other countries. The cost of such shifts would largely be paid by the federal government. Existing government contracts normally specified where the work would be performed. If the government wished to change the sites of production, this would cause a breach of the agreement, so the DOD would have to pay for the relocations.

CHAPTER 15

PINEHURST, A LUXURY golf resort in North Carolina, offers a respite to corporate executives from their allegedly hectic business lives.

"Well, I thought that since most of the board members play golf, why not meet at a golf resort," said a smiling Gene Sperling as he lined up his practice putt. Yes, he thought, two days to unwind and relax here, and then they will be feeling no pain when the board meeting is held. Only three items to be covered, and the Anniston move would be approved before they finished their second cups of coffee.

The corporate jet had delivered the board members along with their wives, or significant others, only a few hours ago, and already the men were either on the practice tee or the putting green to warm up before tomorrow's eighteen-hole play, which would be followed by a Southern-style barbecue dinner. Copious amounts of alcohol would be readily available throughout the festivities.

Gene had orchestrated the entire three days with the guidance of an events coordinator at Pinehurst. Nothing was being left to chance. All of it was intended to deliver the board members to a short meeting on the last morning where a vote on the move to China would take place.

Back in New York, Ira Horowitz, the company's general counsel, who did not play golf, was reading through a legal newsletter. He planned to fly down to North Carolina the afternoon before the board meeting, but at the moment his eyes were drawn to an article entitled "Government Contracting and Security." It seemed that an executive order would now prevent certain militarily related products from being manufactured outside of the United States. Although details were lacking, Ira realized that this could potentially impact the company's operations, and he needed to know more ASAP.

A quick call to the company's principal Washington, DC, law firm led to the usual disclaimer whenever new rules were first announced: "We don't know yet. It's too early to speculate. We need to see those regulations to spell out the details of how it's to be interpreted."

Ira realized, based upon similar prior experiences, that his duty was to warn the key decision-makers about this item and recommend they postpone any decisions that might be affected by it. His next call was to Gene's cell, which was at that moment in the Pinehurst Club bar.

Gene replied, "We can't slow this thing down now because of a potential legal hurdle that may not even exist."

"A short postponement for a month or two would be prudent under the circumstances," Ira replied, but Gene had already hung up. A frustrated Ira had been in this position before with Gene. OK, I've done my job, thought Ira as he shrugged his shoulders and left for another meeting on an unrelated item.

Claire and George were not overly concerned about the board meeting in North Carolina. Just the perks of executive privilege, thought Claire. Her work had been done, and, yes, she thought, there had now been sufficient factual input to make an intelligent decision.

Einar, who was preparing for a trip to Anniston, was less sanguine as he realized that the board members could be manipulated particularly in a laid-back, isolated environment such as Pinehurst, even though all relevant facts were on the table. There was no guarantee that the board would be fully informed before making their decision. He had a flight to catch to keep a promise to the employees in Alabama to tell them the real scoop, but now he wondered what he should tell them.

Gene was glad that he had not brought his new girlfriend, Sonja, as she probably would not charm the board members' wives with whom she would be associating. It also left him free to micromanage this event.

Meanwhile the company's Washington law firm had swung into high gear. Influencing the writing of regulations was their bread and butter. Billable hours generated by strategy sessions and commenting on proposed regulations would add up quickly. The young lawyers in the government agencies usually welcomed this input because they often did not understand the industries that they were supposed to be regulating, and they also wanted to curry the favor of future potential employers.

Gene was worried that Ira would be in Pinehurst tomorrow and would likely mention this new legal development to the board in an effort to protect himself from future criticism.

At nine the next morning, the golfing members started their rounds of golf on legendary Pinehurst #2, which had recently been the site of both the men's and women's US Open Championships. The weather was clear with temperatures in the low eighties with relatively high humidity. Despite using electric carts, these older men would be tired in four hours when they came back into the clubhouse.

The next day Gene woke early, dressed in a sporty collared golf shirt with matching slacks and confidently strode into the breakfast room where his show was about to begin. The other board members began to shuffle in, looking somewhat groggy after the golf and the late-night barbecue dinner.

"Gentlemen, please grab some breakfast and settle around the large table in the next room, and we can get started," Gene said with a warm smile.

"Today, we have a chance to hit a home run for our shareholders," he began when everyone was finally seated. The lights were dimmed so the screen could be seen in sharper focus.

"We are here for one purpose only: to make the best decisions for the owners of our business. Our company has overcome challenges in the past to become a leader in the industry. Today, we face unprecedented competition, which threatens our very existence," he opened.

Gene used the remote to manipulate his PowerPoint. "This graph, with projections of sales and profits, illustrates my point. Notice that those companies that relocated operations overseas not only showed increased profits, but also picked up additional sales abroad. The next slide, based upon our own internal analysis, indicates that we could expect similar results."

He closed by saying, "Gentlemen, we are operating in a global marketplace whether we want to acknowledge it or not."

At that moment, Ira Horowitz, who had arrived at Pinehurst late the night before, rose from the table and agreed that Gene's presentation was accurate, but that other factors needed to be considered.

Open conflicts during board meetings were rare. Normally differences were ironed out beforehand. Thus, the typically congenial atmosphere quickly faded as the board members seemed to reach a more alert state.

With all eyes now on Ira, he began a brief presentation that he had rehearsed mentally on the flight to North Carolina.

"First, and foremost, our largest customer is the US government, which constitutes over half of our annual sales. Of that amount, roughly half involves military-related products. Production of those products is likely to be limited to manufacturing solely in the US under regulations that are under active consideration as we speak. Production at Anniston is almost entirely directed to meet military contracts," Ira said.

Gene, sensing that he was losing the momentum that he had so carefully cultivated, said, "Ira, thanks for bringing this concern to our attention, but as we all know, there always seems to be some legal impediment, real or imagined, to our making business decisions."

Ira sat down, having made his point, but the other board members began talking among themselves.

Finally, Bill Harnett, the CEO of a large publicly traded agricultural commodities company and senior board member, stood and said, "Gene, I have heard about those new rules that Ira mentioned, and those regulations are real. They will be issued soon. Given their potential impact, we can't proceed with this item today."

The others slowly nodded in agreement.

Gene knew that it would be futile for him to continue. He quickly moved to the two other items on the agenda, and they were promptly resolved, which allowed him to gain some cover on his embarrassment with the first item.

Just before his departure for Alabama, Einar had received a call from Ira conveying the same information. Yes, he thought, there is some hope I can give the plant guys. When he took a second call, at the airport from Ira, his mood brightened further. The plant relocation had been withdrawn from the agenda.

CHAPTER 16

THE CHINESE DELEGATION in Washington was now also aware of these pending rules and was convening a meeting with their lobbyists in Washington. The Chinese commercial attaché set the tone, "Once again the US government is leaning away from friendly relations with China. We want to be sure that American firms have the opportunity to expand their operations in China for our mutual benefit. We want you to quickly find a way to stop these new regulations before they are made final. We know that you have the knowledge and connections to make that happen."

The six men in custom-tailored suits and two elegantly coiffured ladies knew they would now have to earn their exorbitant fees. Who exactly was assigned to write these regulations and what guidance had that person received beyond the vaguely worded presidential decree? How accessible would these people be? They had to get "access" quickly.

Up in New York, Claire was receiving a phone call from a fellow Dartmouth "tuckie."

"Brad Jameson, so nice to hear from you," she responded.

"I'm in the city for a few days and hoped that we might have lunch or something and catch up."

"I'd enjoy that," she said enthusiastically. "I'll be interested to hear about the world of consulting and swap news about our fellow classmates."

George happened to be out of town on another audit, and things were slow at corporate headquarters. Claire met Brad at the

Swiss Center for lunch at two the next afternoon thinking that the place would be less crowded at that time.

"Claire, let me be up front with you. I just lost my job and am in town on a job search."

"My God, Brad, what happened? You were among those most likely to succeed!"

"The atmosphere was like a snake pit. My assignments were often ill defined, sometimes trying to bring life into companies that were too far gone to revive. My boss was no help. He blamed me for not being able to do the impossible. We had a few arguments, and then two weeks ago I got my pink slip. I've come to the conclusion that consulting is not for me. Now I'm hoping to find a spot with more security, less stress, and at least some free time." Brad looked at Claire for a reaction.

"Brad, my job here started out with a bang. I had interactions with senior executives in the first few days, but soon I found myself in the middle of titanic struggles, and the stress continues to intensify. Frankly, the bloom is off the rose, but I'm hanging in there to see what happens next. Who knows, maybe things will get better. I don't know of any positions in our company that might be a fit at the moment, but I'll keep on the lookout for you."

"Thanks, but I guess our expectations coming out of Dartmouth may have been too idealistic. If nothing turns up within six months, I may join my family's home construction business. That's beginning to look better every day."

"Wish I could be more encouraging, Brad, but I'm sure you'll find your niche, and all of this will seem like a bad dream."

After the luncheon, Brad went to visit some headhunter recruitment firms, and Claire returned to her office. *Maybe I did make the right career choice*, she thought. *It certainly seems better than the situation that Brad has gone through.*

Claire had decided to resume her exploration of the city, but not alone, remembering her previous exploration that had led to her unsavory adventure in Brighton Beach with the Russian immigrants. I'll take a city tour and then the boat cruise around Manhattan, she decided. It would be fun, safe, and relaxing. While mixing with the tourists as a city resident, she realized that she knew more about the city than she had realized.

Meanwhile, important news was being delivered in Alabama. "No, I'm not telling you that the move depends on words written in some technical government regulation, but only that is why the board put off making a decision," said Einar to a gathering of factory employees.

"Everything will continue on here as it has been for now, and I'll keep you updated. That's the best I can do," he said. "Look," he continued, "we are a pawn in a global struggle. Most Asian countries are now fully aware of the importance of foreign investment for economic growth, updating technology, and reducing unemployment. Much like the individual states in the United States, which compete against each other to attract business, this competition among Asian countries had become fierce. Our company cannot simply opt out of this game. We must be involved in it or we will soon be out of business. Specialty Chemicals has no choice but to be a global competitor."

Later, meeting privately in the plant manager's office with some key employees, Einar explained how the board was viewing the situation. "Tax holidays and cheap labor are a big lure for some businesses such as clothing manufacturers, but lax environmental laws are more attractive to chemical manufacturers like us. US companies lost an advantage when this country initiated environmental laws. Losing this advantage has led to our businesses becoming less competitive. This is how our board sees things."

"I get it," said Bill Vaalens, the plant manager, "but the rank and file think that headquarters doesn't give a shit about them."

Einar continued, "When I was working here we were just beginning to deal with environmental problems. Hopefully the waste problem from that VX toxic chemical we made for the Army has been solved, but even now we are facing water pollution problems that arose from Anniston's operations. The potential cost of dealing with all of this is astronomical. That, plus tax costs compels the board to consider a relocation. If they didn't consider it, the shareholders, who own this company would force the issue."

He continues, "I've read that China and South Korea have recently taken a longer-term approach. Factory assets that are outdated or lack modern quality controls will not serve national interests and, therefore, might not be allowed to be imported. Asia consists principally of export-driven economies as opposed to the predominantly consumer-based economies of Western Europe and the United States. This difference has given Asian countries a voracious appetite for foreign investments that its own capital markets cannot yet provide. These Asian countries want the employment and wealth generating potential that comes with it."

The plant supervisors thanked Einar for having the guts to come down and tell them the true reality of the situation.

The high stakes and carefully orchestrated sales pitch at Pinehurst had backfired on Gene, and the deferral of the relocation decision was generating many rumors.

Three days later Einar called a meeting of his headquarters staff.

"Gene has pretty much lost the confidence of the other board members, and we may be looking for a new CEO before long," said Einar. "When the other board members found out that he knew about those proposed defense contracting regulations before his sales pitch in Pinehurst, they lost their trust in him. This information is not for publication. It's only my reading of the tea leaves. The real reason that I called this meeting is that I want you all to know, at the same time, that I am putting my papers in for retirement at the end of the month."

The staffers looked at each other in shock.

Einar went on, "New York City has never really been my cup of tea, but I will miss all of you."

Einar's staff at corporate headquarters consisted of twelve employees, who worked closely with the company's nine plant locations. They all sat in stunned silence, Claire among them. The announcement was unexpected.

Einar finally continued, "The plant managers will be receiving my news in a conference call later today. At the moment there has been no decision about my replacement."

Claire felt as if the ground had moved under her feet. First, Einar was her boss, then they were on opposite sides. Eventually, they worked together again—all in the space of less than a year. Maybe I've had enough of this corporate rat race, she thought.

By midafternoon, rumors were flying, and the company stock price had taken a dive. The next day an article in the *Wall Street Journal* speculated that the company might soon be "in play" meaning that it could be the subject of a take-over by some corporate raider or perhaps be split into several smaller companies. These type of rumors quickly affected employee morale, customer relations, credit ratings, and even the value of stock-option-type compensation.

The *Wall Street Journal* article had not been missed by the Chinese embassy staff in Washington. Much as the Chinese company Lenovo was overtaking IBM in sales in the computer industry, other companies were also either being acquired or losing business to Chinese firms. Beijing's policy was moving forward to acquire companies around the world that might further their interests. Perhaps an American chemical company could be a desirable candidate.

George heard the news about Einar's retirement and Gene's loss of support from Claire in a phone call that afternoon. She also mentioned that she might start looking around.

"Maybe something outside of the city would be a better lifestyle," she said.

The public relations department was now in high gear, responding to both media and shareholder questions. Anything to quell the speculation. Gene, meanwhile, even with his PR background, was astonished at the speed that this frenzy had gripped the company.

The move to China as a top priority had now been replaced with bare survival, but an idea was forming. He might offer his resignation in an effort to calm the turmoil, if the board would offer a reasonable severance package. Hell, he thought, it could be a better deal than the money he would have made if the move overseas had gone forward.

His bargaining position with the board was slipping away, so he would need to move quickly.

He didn't know the board had already held a short meeting and decided against a package of any kind for Gene in exchange for his resignation.

CHAPTER 17

"Why meet up there?" asked Claire, when she took a phone call from George.

"Because it's the most romantic place I can think of. The movies *An Affair to Remember* and *Sleepless in Seattle* enshrined it in my memory," replied George, who was a big movie fan. He had recently started to show this other side of himself. She liked it.

Claire guessed that maybe this was his way of giving her a heads up that he wanted to formalize their relationship in a traditional way. Was she really ready for this? Maybe in six months things would be more settled. Now there were uncertainties about her job; maybe it was too soon; did she really wish to put down roots in the Big Apple? Maybe she could put him off gently.

Bill Harnett, the board member who had challenged Gene, was at this moment sitting by himself at a small table in the bar at the Waldorf Astoria. Einar knew that this was no invitation for a social chat when he sat down in the opposite chair.

"Einar, we need to turn this thing around and fast. I had a meeting over the weekend with the rest of the board at my place in the Hamptons, and we decided that radical steps need to be taken."

Einar sat silently wondering where this was going, particularly since he had just applied for retirement.

"Those new Defense Department contracting regulations make it clear that a move to China would gut our whole defense business. Gene's got to go, but we also must make other changes that will say to the media and shareholders that the company knows where it's headed. Confidence needs to be restored," Bill said.

Einar was bracing himself. "Maybe a bold move like moving the headquarters out of Manhattan, for example, might help persuade people that we are not just another old-line company. Einar, we are willing to make a big bet that you're the guy who can put the company on the right track."

Einar was momentarily stunned with this expression of confidence from the board. All he could think to say was, "Are you serious?"

"Hell, yes, we're serious. You've been with the company for a long time, and you have the trust and respect of the entire organization. Your compensation would match Gene's package, but we would expect you to stay for at least another year."

"My wife, Sandra, is in North Carolina right now looking for retirement housing. Obviously I'll need to discuss it with her," replied Einar.

"You do that, and call me within three or four days with your decision."

Then Bill was gone. Einar stayed to think and nurse his whiskey and soda. How would Sandra react after all their talk about enjoying a happy future retirement?

That evening Einar reached Sandra at her hotel in Cary, North Carolina. "Find any interesting places yet?" he ventured first.

"A few that you should come and look at," she responded.

"Maybe we should put it off because the board has asked me to consider taking the helm as CEO, and I told them I'd check with you," he casually replied.

After a rather long pause, she said, "I didn't think you were ready for retirement just yet, despite your statements to the contrary. I've stuck with you for thirty-four years now, and I have no regrets. Besides, if you're the CEO, those other executive wives will now have to kowtow to me. They've never accepted me as one of their group, and it would, frankly, be fun to be the queen bee of that group."

Sandra grinned at the prospect. Finally she concluded by saying, "You should do it, and I'll back you up, if you really want it."

Later that night, on the observation deck of the Empire State Building, Claire approached George, who had arrived first. Both were smiling and looking somewhat unsure.

"Need I spell this out for you, Claire, or will you save me the awkward moment of asking you directly," said George without making eye contact and sounding rather nervous.

"Yes, George, you must say it all directly to me because this is a moment that I want to remember."

Slowly George opened a small box containing a diamond ring. Two minutes later the couple was kissing, crying, and laughing. The stars of the night sky and the electric lights of the city below seemed to be signaling their approval.

Several days later Einar communicated his acceptance of the board's offer, Gene was quietly informed that his services would no longer be required. Gene Sperling had sensed for several weeks that any further efforts by him to revive the China relocation issue would be doomed. There would be no bonus from the company and certainly not from the Chinese.

No press releases mentioned Gene by name, but they did state that a longtime employee, Einar Horne, would lead the company into the future. The following day the stock rebounded. Einar began to renew the confidence of customers and shareholders.

CHAPTER 18

Soon things began to settle down at the Company, and the newly engaged couple began to think about their big day. The first problem was money. Claire wanted to liquidate her student loans as soon as possible and help pay for her brother's rehab expenses. Her MBA training led her to set these priorities over a onetime event. The honeymoon would have to be deferred because George was in the midst of tax season at work.

"Claire, did you know that couples who have expensive weddings get divorced more often than those who have more modest weddings?" George told her.

"No, George, I did not know that, and probably you are making it up." "Actually," he said, "there is research on the subject, and it was reported in a magazine I read recently."

George should have known that Claire had a clear idea of exactly what she wanted. He had no preconception or strong opinion as to the ceremony itself, so he wisely accepted her concept.

"George, it will be a small, but elegant wedding in St. Patrick's in Natick where I was baptized and received my first Holy Communion. We will have a modest reception directly across the street in a park where there is a bandstand. It will be more like a picnic, but elegant. When I was a little girl, I saw a couple having their wedding reception there." "It was so perfect that that is a dream I still have for myself."

"There is no research to my knowledge about any correlations between the cost of a reception and a divorce, however," reported

George with a sly grin, as if to say that a more expensive reception might be OK, if the ceremony itself were modest.

George was bowled over by the way Claire had visualized the whole thing in such detail. Her brother, Arne, would walk her down the aisle, and a girlfriend from Dartmouth would be her bridesmaid. She hoped too, that George and Arne would become friends.

George asked his father to be his best man, but his whole family of eight would be part of the entourage. Since George was a member of the Greek Orthodox Church, his family had wanted the ceremony at their local church on Staten Island, but Claire's strong vision won the day. Her family had been staunch members of St. Pat's, and so with confidence she called her childhood parish and asked for Father Cullen.

"Do you remember me? I'm Claire Perkins from the parish."

"Of course, I remember you lass, the tall one with the flaming red hair. How are you and why do I happen to have the pleasure of speaking with you today?" Father Cullen asked.

First, the hair is now brown and I am calling to say that I want to get married in St. Pat's with you doing the ceremony."

"I'm flattered and honored to be asked by the likes of you, but may I ask a few questions first?"

They discussed dates, music to be played, and the estimated size of the gathering. Claire described George's Greek Orthodox affiliation, which did not seem to disturb Father Cullen.

With most details readily agreeable to St. Pat's, Claire made her next call to Natick City Hall and asked about using the city park for the reception.

"Can't completely close the park," she was told, "but for a few hours in the afternoon, you can use half of the park and the bandstand." The city authorized the gathering in the park for three hours for up to twenty-five people, which Claire thought would be adequate.

A small band that Arne knew would play music carefully selected by Claire in the park's bandstand. A van was rented for the New York attendees for the trip north.

Fortunately, the weather, which was a big "if," was glorious, and the event fulfilled Claire's vision.

After changing back into normal clothes from her short wedding dress, she had one final nostalgic wish. "I want a hot dog at Casey's, which has been a local landmark eatery since 1922."

George took her there before they drove back to New York later the same day, arriving at their new apartment in Greenwich Village late that evening. The new apartment was, of course, walking distance from the Greek restaurant that was George's family base in the city.

"Hey, Claire," said George in a phone call on a Monday afternoon two weeks later. "I've been asked to go to a three-day tax seminar in Washington next week, and I've never been there. Have you?"

"Yes, a high school class trip, about ten years ago."

"Would you like to go back?" "To a tax seminar? Not really," replied Claire trying to be funny.

"You know what I mean. Maybe we could go there for our honeymoon. My firm would pay for my travel and hotel room, and then we could extend it a few days and see Washington. There is the Kennedy Center, the Smithsonian, and lots of historical stuff."

"Actually, I would like to compare their Metro to our subway system and see if ours is as bad as people say, or if DC's is that much better," Claire teased. George laughed. "I wonder how many people would go to Washington on their honeymoon to compare public subway systems," he replied.

"It would save a bundle, and, hey, it's a honeymoon, so it doesn't much matter where we end up," said Claire. They would have Friday evening, the weekend, and Monday morning for their honeymoon.

After riding the Amtrak to Washington by himself on this first visit to the city, George walked out of Union Station and gazed at Capitol Hill. He decided to pass up a taxi and walked back into the station because he wanted to get a feel for DC's much newer subway system which was two levels below.. Coming back up to daylight two blocks from his hotel, he had to admit that the Metro seemed better in almost every way, but he recognized too that it was built a hundred years later than New York's.

His tax seminar was held in a huge conference room in the Mayflower Hotel's first floor. The theme was "Recent Changes in US Taxation of International Transactions." Washington hosted such programs every time legislation was passed that impacted big companies or whenever the courts interpreted the arcane language in the Internal Revenue Code in a new way. The speakers were typically partners from prominent law and accounting firms who were hoping to advertise their talents to prospective new clients.

Claire was scheduled to arrive the next evening, and she would sight-see while he labored through the last day of the seminar. They would have the weekend to enjoy the city and each other. Claire's train slowed to a stop right on time Thursday night. They met at the train and embraced as if they had been apart for years rather than days. It now seemed like light-years since they had first gotten acquainted en route to a factory in Alabama about a year ago.

Since both had eaten dinner earlier, George suggested going to a few watering holes in nearby Georgetown because he wanted to compare nightlife in DC to that in NYC. Claire laughed, recognizing that this comparison was similar to her interest in comparing subways.

He told her, "I've already made the subway comparison and DC wins, hands down. You'll need to trust me on that because the Metro doesn't go into Georgetown."

They found Georgetown quaint, a bit touristy, but the bars were more crowded than those in Manhattan would be on a Thursday evening. Walking into Mr. Smith's, a well-established hangout for the young and upwardly mobile on M Street, Claire found herself staring into a familiar face from far away, but now leaning against the bar five feet from her.

"Colin Dunlop, what are you doing here?"

"I should ask the same of you. Did the New Yorkers run you out of town?"

After introducing George and Colin, the threesome decided to find a more quiet spot because this popular bar was crowded—and noisy. Settling into a more subdued atmosphere down the street, Claire explained how she knew Colin. "So why are you here?" asked Claire. "No, you first, why are you here?" replied Colin in his clipped British accent. Claire filled him in on her corporate work and new husband.

Colin, filling in the gap since they had worked together, had developed a network of American business contacts from his job in Hong Kong, helping them evaluate business opportunities in China, much as he had done with Claire's company. That led to an opportunity at the British Embassy in Washington. He was now in his second month here.

An hour later, George and Claire left Colin to go to their hotel, but Claire agreed to meet Colin the next day for lunch because George would be busy with his seminar.

"I really can't believe this," Claire said, when they met the next day. "It truly is a small world." "So, I'm all ears," Colin said. "Did your company move the plant to China? After I filed a report about it, I lost track."

"No, the whole thing fell apart because Gene, the CEO who was pushing the move, lost the trust of the board. A change in US government regulations also had a lot to do with the decision to stay put."

"Claire, did you ever wonder why you were asked to contact us in Hong Kong?"

"Not really. I guess I was so tired at that point that I was just trying to complete my assignment and write a report. But now that I think about it, there must have been something going on behind the scenes."

"There was indeed. I can tell you what I know," Colin said. "Your company had been on our radar screen ever since your former CEO, Gene somebody, started making an investigation in China about a possible plant relocation there. When you came over, we decided to ask your company if we might help you avoid being misled. What's the situation with that plant now, if I might ask?"

"It's still operating, although a small part that was dealing with some secret air force contract has been shut down."

"Actually, Claire, I know something about that from my new job here in Washington," Colin said.

"Please, do tell," she responded with great curiosity.

"First, the US Air Force reactivated a contract that the army had canceled at Anniston. This type of activity is sometimes called a false flags operation—meaning that it was not what it appeared to be. Under the air force, it operated for a short period of time. In essence, it was a counter-intelligence operation to try to find out who and how anyone might try to steal military technology, so we could learn more about their operations and better protect the technology. More I cannot say."

"Colin, you always have amazing things to tell me. George and I had just decided to explore DC upscale bars and compare them to those in New York City when we ran into you. There seems to be a lot going on behnd the scenes that I am not understanding."

"Actually Claire you already know more than your government would like. It's my job to swap intelligence information on behalf of Her Majesty's government with the US and similar services of other countries. There, now you know even more than you should, but I'll not go any further than that."

"Now back to your comparison of bars. Let me help you out with that, because my job finds me in New York from time to time, and here's how I see the differences so far. In New York, it's the same age group, but they're mostly hard-driving junior business professionals. But in DC, there're more public-policy dilettantes drawn to the political scene. The drink prices are about the same, though. The most fun, however, continues to be the pubs in England."

"Thanks for that penetrating analysis, Colin, but what practical success have you made of all of that research?"

"I'll leave that to your imagination, my dear," he replied with a boyish grin.

The honeymoon, short though it was, went well. Breakfast in bed at noon followed an evening of passion, which had left the couple sated. Her inhibitions, indoctrinated by her Catholic upbringing, had soon given way to a pent-up need that she didn't know she had.

They returned to New York and settled into the lifestyle in which married professionals in New York usually find themselves. The bar scene was no longer an element in their lives, but riding those New York subway trains remained part of their daily life. A move to a real home in a real neighborhood would soon be their goal with the trade-off of accepting a much longer commute.

Several months earlier, in a research facility in China, nuclear weapons experts reluctantly concluded that a supposed micro-nuclear warhead stolen from America contained no nuclear material. Apparently the cylinder was something other than a warhead. It was assumed that the graduate chemistry student must have mistakenly taken the wrong cylinder.

About the Author

TOM WILLIAMS WAS an officer in the US Army's Fourth Infantry Division after graduating from Ranger school. He worked in the international division of a multinational company and also in Washington, DC, and overseas with the US government. Williams holds both MBA and juris doctor degrees. He graduated from the University of Notre Dame in 1963.

Tom resides in Cary, North Carolina and can be reached by e-mail at <tfwill41@gmail.com>

Made in the USA
Columbia, SC
24 October 2024